pikeSpike

pikeSpike

❖ ❖ ❖

Hobhouse 18

ISBN: 1519415060
ISBN 13: 9781519415066
Library of Congress Control Number: 2015919402
CreateSpace Independent Publishing Platform
North Charleston, South Carolina

Prologue

❖ ❖ ❖

A FIGURE DRESSED HEAD TO toe in black walks carefully down a narrow street. He picks up his feet to avoid horse droppings or vomit, tutting to himself in a thin voice. When a wagon comes past, nearly brushing him, loaded with fire-wood and straw, he squeaks and mutters, 'oh dear, oh dear, oh dear'.

The doors of the drinking houses emit belches of raucous noise and a stench which has the man wrinkling his nose and speeding up his careful feet.

Finally, sighing, he reaches the last drinking establishment of the street, benches and tables spilling onto a patch of dirty grass. There is a bit of sunshine on the scarred pine table top but that is smeared off by a huge woman and her filthy cloth.

'Yes, vicar, what'll it be?' she tries a smile and her gold tooth glints.

'Oh dear, oh dear', the vicar mutters, hardly meeting her eye or her tooth, 'I have an appointment but I suppose I could perchance try a mug of your best cider?'

'There's only one and it's slop. Try the sack'.

'All right, Mrs Brownlow. I suppose I shall be at the back' and he makes an even more cautious way to a table right at the back, hidden by the roof eaves. But even as his feet avoid spills and rubbish, find some cracked paving, his eyes are darting here and there behind his eyeglasses. When he finally sits, groaning at the effort and muttering 'oh dear, oh dear', he positions himself to watch the other customers and the road.

Completely hidden under the eaves, only a voice emerges. 'A very strange place you have brought me to'. The landlady plonks a small glass of sherry on the table and waddles away, shouting. The voice continues - 'very strange indeed. However, you say that you might have something for me'.

'I have two boys'.

'Boys, really?'

'I know it sounds unlikely. Their names are Bowman and Appleton'.

'Any relation to Sir William Bowman?'

'Nephew'.

'All right, I'll have them sent round to me. I've got the right sort of chap to look after them. Could be excellent'. The man smiles but the smile does not reach his eyes.

'If you need me, call for me'. The man in black rises, remembers that he is an old man and slowly picks his way out of the cider-house. The war has just started - last year - but there was little sign of it here. The boats and barges are being unloaded at the four busy wharves. The dockers - always the noisiest of men - are shouting as usual. The carts stream away from the wharves either clogging up the narrow high street or, more commonly, out towards Taunton and the far West. The Vicar smiles a wintry sort of smile and begins slowly walking back up the High Street.

CHAPTER 1
Pike Men

❖ ❖ ❖

HE THOUGHT, 'THE MOMENT HAS come'.

He picked up his pike and walked away. He laughed for no reason as he joined the road. There was, to start with, nobody on it. But then he spotted his friend Ned and shouted, 'Ned, Ned'. Ned shouted softly back.

They'd told their families and Ned's Mum had told him not to go. They'd argued for days until finally she'd given in. Ned's dad had not been heard of for many a day. His own family had been cross but allowed him. 'You're sixteen now. You do what you want'. But behind their hard words there were tears. His mother was in the garden when he'd left.

The boys met under the limes near the church. The church bell rang once and they both looked up and then smiled at each other. Ned was a bit shorter, his hair dark. When she was in a good mood, his mum called him a little Celt. They rested their pikes against the tree and Ned began to bundle them together like he'd seen the soldiers do. Two pikes were easier to carry than one.

'Yours has come out a proper job', George told his friend who flushed with pride.

Further on, he laughed again. Ned looked at him with a question in his green eyes. 'It's not usually these pike I carry', he said.

Ned laughed too but a bit nervously. They'd gone fishing together dozens of times. It was what they did. Last year, the pike had saved both their families. This year the pike would destroy them – at least that's what Ned's mum declared in their loudest argument. She'd not called him a 'little Celt' then

Ned himself was a quiet lad. He could remember when the vicar had them both at Sunday school and had spent the first hour or so thinking that Ned was touched or slow. Funny to remember that today, he thought.

'George, George', Ned said as loud as he ever managed. Ned had suddenly dropped their bags in the dust. 'George, there are people'.

'You don't say', he answered not moving the pikes from his shoulder and watching a raggle-taggle group walk up the road from Low Ham. There was one man on a horse. 'Now watch yourself with Billy-boy'. Ned despite everything, his quietness, his serious face, would fight with their school-mate Billy at the drop of a hat. George need not have worried. Billy-boy looked green as an unripe apple.

The man on the horse spoke to them from his great height. 'Well done brave lads. Are the Rowswells coming too?'

'I'm sorry squire, I haven't seen 'em' George kicked at the road.

'G'wan, get on with you', the man shouted but it was at his horse who'd started nibbling at the verge. George looked at the animal with a professional eye.

'I'd like as not end up a farrier', he thought, like his dad. His dad had put expensive iron shoes on this beast here and declared, 'not enough bone there'. If his dad said it, it was true: at least where horses were concerned. His father, George had only realised recently when he'd been allowed down the pub for the first time, his dad could talk nonsense with the best of them. And, in all honesty, the best of them included Squire Latham, who was smiling at him fondly.

'Those are right beauties', he declared. The four or five boys with him laughed. 'The pikes, you bunch of clod-hoppers'.

'Ned, he's no beauty', Billy found the courage to say. His colour had returned, from green to bright red in an instant. Like George himself, Billy had the slightly reddy-blond straggle of coarse hair typical for a 'local'. Round Henley, the Peppard lot had hair almost white and, strangely, Billy's mum was a Peppard. That made Billy a second cousin of his – at least that's what the vicar said.

Beside him, Ned swore and was about to react when the Squire addressed him by name, 'Ned Appleton, your mum came round to your way of thinking?'

'Not really, sir' and spat on the verge. 'Best get on!' he said to George.

'We'm gathering at Huish, with Sir David Wilson'. George offered, politely.

'Indeed', the squire said, 'so you are'.

Not without some pleasure, Ned and George swung away across the fields. 'Come on', shouted George and his shorter friend trotted to keep up. At the site of the old Roman villa, in Farmer Ainscott's field (long ago it had been an Appleton field so Ned had long regarded it as 'really his') they sat awhile. The pikes had rubbed at George's shoulder through the thick leather of his jerkin. Truth be told, neither was very eager to be at the muster. They could have gone with the Squire easy but he wasn't their squire. That was the whole point of High Ham. It was a 'free' village. As volunteer pikemen, George and Ned got a much better deal than those yokels with Billy-boy. Also, George was a bit afraid of his friend. He looked at him now.

'You'll be alright', he told Ned as they ate the last of last year's apples and spat the pips on their (new-ish) boots. The truth was, and George was fully aware of it, he kept close to Ned not to protect him.

'He's a berserker', the vicar had told him last year. The vicar had been kind enough to speak up for George and Ned at the local magistrates. It had been, funnily enough, when they'd been fetching the pikes from Aller woods. Normally, neither George nor Ned would have been fool enough to get caught napping. Happened though, they'd 'borrowed' some cider from George's dad and were sleeping off their head-aches when they'd been jumped on. In the first whirl-wind of punches, George had thought they'd be set on by gypsies. 'They have become even more lawless', the vicar had told the magistrate.

That was the excuse for Ned's behaviour. Everyone knew that gypsies would knife you for a penny. (Actually, even though they had bought their unfinished pike-heads from Gypsy Hughes at Curry Rival, no gypsy would expect a penny from either of them. Hughes had been surprised by the shilling for the pike spikes. The lads looked like what they were, country boys growing to manhood, no coins on them for months at a time).

Ned had damned near killed them all. In fact, if George hadn't dragged him away, he thought Ned would certainly have killed at least one. Fully grown men. Of course, George figured as he watched his new-ish high boots nearly a foot long waggle around in the sunshine, he himself was, now, bloody close to full grown.

He remembered the fight. While George had been lying half-stunned, scrumpy vomit hot in his throat and an apprentice from Langport on his chest, he had watched amazed as Ned had begun flying around the natural clearing. He'd picked up one of the pike shafts, thwacked the bloke on top of George (he keeled over without a murmur) and took on the other three with his bare hands. One of them produced a knife. It was really like flying. Ned, shouting and swearing still softly, white flecks of rage round his mouth, leapt <u>over</u> the man with the knife. In passing, he'd put a finger in the man's eye and torn it.

One of the other men shouted something daft like, 'I'm not having that' and ran at little Ned. Ned stood there snarling, more dog than boy and had seized and bitten the hand raised to him. Without letting go, he ripped off the man's ear and kicked him again and again in the balls. When the other man came close, again like a dog, Ned raked his claws across his neck, damaging his wind-pipe. George had pulled himself together from where he lay and pulled Ned off the bitten man. It was hard enough to get him to undo his teeth-clench. It was well-nigh impossible to stop Ned attacking him as well. They'd left a welter a blood and moans in the clearing but they'd taken their pike shafts, already bloodied. George was sick a few times more on the way home. And not just from the cider.

George had told the vicar. Old Muthers and Young Muthers, father and son, both over sixty, had gone over to the Woods and, luckily for George and Ned, found no dead bodies. A complaint had been placed with the magistrate. No one looking at the quiet Ned was going to believe it. 'We'll get you yet', the half-blinded apprentice had promised outside the hearing before seeing Ned coming and disappearing sharp-ish.

They got up in the field. 'We'm best be pushing on', Ned smiled, as though remembering that fight. He'd had plenty since. In fact, and only George knew this, he'd been thinking of becoming a fighter, maybe at fairs or in Bristol.

They walked in the shade of the two new houses at Paradise, built by ardent Parliamentarians. The little apples were green on the trees. Not so very long to harvest, George thought, not so long 'til the fairs came again, if there ever were fairs again.

'Stupid war', Ned said, as if reading his mind. He added a swear word or two. 'Stupid bloody war'. Ned took the pikes off George and carried them as though they were weightless.

CHAPTER 2

Iron Side Men

❖ ❖ ❖

THEY CRESTED THE RISE KNOWN as Bowden's after Bowden's Farm over to their right. Below was the view well known to them. The bustling port of Langport. The River Parrott. The bits and bobs of flooded levels. Smoke from the houses along the high street, and from the wharves, hung in the still sunny air. There were unusual knots of people gathering here and there, not like market day, more like the elections.

It was a man-made landscape. Even in these war years the river was dredged, the rhines re-dug, the ditches cleared. There was always a bit of flooding – indeed the spillage from the river seemed to make the fields exceptionally fertile. When not fishing for pike to sell to rich people, Ned and George were often scouring the levels for wild-fowl. That was how George had come by his unusual skills and equipment.

They turned left a bit, Huish church visible a mile or two away, and were about to go down-hill through an old orchard.

A cry from behind stopped them. At first, they thought it was a very tall man. Gradually, they realised it was a very tall boy. Decked out in enormous hat, feather, what looked like a piece of armour and an actual sword which seemed intent on tripping him up, he raised his hand again 'wait a second, lads'.

Even this seemed to annoy George. 'Nathanial, we'll not walk with you if you are going to fight with the roundheads and your namesake'.

'Of course I'm fighting with you, what do you take me for?'

Ned chose to take this question seriously, 'a weird French puritan with Parliamentary parents'.

'Ho ho ho', Nate laughed a deep, contagious laugh but the other boys did not join in. They were still staring at him with anger. He was the proverbial bean-pole. The metal breast plate was far too big for him and looked extremely old-fashioned. The enormous hat made him look something like a flower.

'All that come from the Armada did it?' Ned asked.

'As opposed to that thing', he pointed to George's weapon.

'If you have to join us, come on!' Ned turned round and deliberately swung the pikes round at head height. At that moment, Nate bent over to adjust his huge cavalier boots and the twelve foot poles whistled past him and would have hit George except he caught them.

'Ow, Ned watch out'. He was given the unusual sight of a smile from his berserker friend.

The hapless Nate was busy striding down through the orchard trees singing 'green grow the apples, oh' tunelessly and Ned with the pikes was following him down when George caught movement at the edge of the trees. He scrambled back up towards Bowden's lane. He could make out two figures on horses.

There was something about them.

Feeling his heart thud, George took the bow off his back, dropped the two packs, and started working his way to the left side of the squat trees. He could make the soldiers out a bit better. They had drawn their swords. Their buff and mustard tops, iron breastplates, made him sure even before their heads with Cromwell's new-fangled 'roundhead' helmet were visible.

He could just make out Nate and Ned approaching where the horsemen stood at silent as statues. Without thinking much at all, George had drawn the bow and loosed three arrows in under a minute. Strangely, both men looked up (he'd made no sound) as the arrows fell on them. Maybe they'd heard the whistle as a foot of local ash (the same ash as the pikes) tipped with a gobbit of sharpened gypsy iron fell through the June air. One of them got the arrow in his mouth, the other in his throat.

'So much for iron sides', George muttered, trying to quell his nausea at killing a man (well, two men). The third arrow had hit a horse. It started bucking and squealing. He'd managed lucky shots before but this was ridiculous.

Even Nate had noticed the commotion. 'What, what, what's that?' George could hear him ask. He grabbed the packs again and allowed his weight to run him down the hill. The ground was squelchy from the recent rain but he did not slip until he was with his friend and Nate.

Ned looked round in the purest admiration. 'You killed them', he whispered in tones of awe and stopped George from falling. George felt sick again, a bit of half-digested apple came into his mouth and he spat it out. The wounded horse had stopped prancing about and had lain down. The dead men lay where they had fallen. There was a silence. George did not want to look at their faces while Ned did not want to stop examining every inch of the 'enemy'. Looking in their pockets.

They were interrupted however by the sound of horses, many horses, and over the rise appeared a whole squadron of cavalry, cantering on the wet ground. George strung an arrow, foolishly – what could he hope to achieve? – but Ned pushed it down. The cavalry were Royalist. A big blonde florid man took off his large, wide-brimmed hat to see them better and looked down from a huge grey horse. 'Vot have ve here?' he asked in a strange foreign accent. The boys did not answer. 'Ach, you got zem vith a bow and arrow'. He looked at George with admiration but, unlike Ned, also a measure of amusement. 'I knew you were backvard in Zummerzet.. ha ha'.

For no reason at all, Nate was laughing too and, then, inexplicably, George, Ned, the whole cavalry troop were guffawing away. Everyone stopped. 'Listen', the foreign man said, 'I must get back to Brizzle but come and see me if you survive ze battle, huh? Your name?'

'I'm George Bowman, your honour'.

'Ah so!' The richly-dressed man turned his horse, said, 'how appropriate' and swept away without a backward glance. A handful of men stayed and a short grim baldie slowly got off his mount.

'Right, these are their forward scouts you so cleverly shot', his voice did not match his face at all, being amused to the point of laughter. And then a grin split his face, to match his voice, and George felt suddenly bathed in attention, like sunshine. Abruptly, he grin went and so did the warmth. 'You and you', he pointed to George and Ned, 'take the rebels' swords. You', he pointed at Nathanial, 'better get on the horse. At least I know that you can ride Nathanial'. The bald man swept a hand over his bald head.

'I am Sir David Wilson and I presume you are mustering with me. Huh?' He seemed to have caught the odd way of questioning off the foreigner. He pointed again – 'George Bowman and ', he pointed again..

'Ned Appleton, sir'.

'Excellent'.

'Excuse me, sir' George found himself asking, 'who be that gentleman?' and pointed the way the blonde man had gone. Perhaps the pointing would go on all day? He thought to himself.

'That, my clever young bowman, was Prince Ruprecht, himself, nephew of the king and commander of the cavalry down here. Now, if you'll excuse me?' he grinned briefly again and got back on his horse. 'Down by the Aller road as quickly as you can, please'.

CHAPTER 3

Club Men

❖ ❖ ❖

THE BOYS WERE DESTINED NEVER to reach the muster. They'd
hardly gone another half a mile, down through Wearne, and
half way down the next hill when another rider appeared. 'Sir
David has changed his mind. He likes the look of you two. You
are to join a foot patrol that will be coming through Wearne
in ten minutes'.

The boys turned round and walked up the hill again, complaining. 'Ten minutes, ten minutes!' Ned joked. 'How'm we
to know what ten minutes be'. (Both of them knew that Ned
was a better time-keeper than any clock ever made).

'Well, for one thing', George answered him, to be annoying, ' we can still see the clock on Huish church'. And they
could. They both turned to look and Ned tried sneakily to hit
George with the butt-end of the pikes. They were also glad to
spend a minute at the horse trough on the way into the hamlet.
It had good, clear water feeding it and they took a moment to

drink deep and dip their heads into the stone vessel. 'I needed that', George laughed and shook a rainbow of drops on the dusty road. He looked at his new sword with real pleasure. He'd never owned a sword before.

An old woman shuffled up towards them. 'You'm playing at soldiers then boys' she said and cackled. 'Nice long pikes you've got too'. She shuffled away still giggling to herself.

Ned looked thoughtfully after her round retreating body. 'She's a witch', he whispered to his friend. 'She gave you the evil eye'.

George laughed very loudly. 'You cannot be serious', he spluttered, water still streaming off his coarse hair. 'The vicar told you there was no such thing often enough'.

'The vicar, the vicar – you bloody love that man', Ned spat out the words, 'think you're so bloody clever'. They might well have come to blows but they were hailed from further down the lane. They turned to face the approaching troop. George was thinking to himself how Ned managed to fight him or Billy without killing them – did that mean he wasn't really a berserker? He looked at Ned's profile and smiled. Nobody could tell how feisty he was just by looking, that was for sure.

Their infantry detachment arrived. 'We're looking for some clubmen', the man in charge finally said. 'Leave your pikes by the hedge and come with us'. Ned easily popped the long wooden objects alongside the blackthorn hedgerow. He missed the look from the last person in the troop. It was one of the apprentices who Ned had thrashed. George had turned round and missed the look too.

'How many club men are there?' he asked the man in charge.

'Sergeant', the burly bloke said.

'How many club men are there, sergeant?'

'Dunno, not a lot, I'm hoping. Can either a you read? Nan of this lot's any help 'tall.'

'We both can read', George said proudly. The sergeant had a strange accent – was it London? Or Hampshire? Neither boy had ever even been to Dorset or Devon. The world was coming to them. George took a bit of cheap parchment from the sergeant and read the scrawl upon it. 'This is from Sir David', he told the big man.

'I know that, you bladdy clod-hopper. What does the blad-dy thing say?'

'It's a passport – to let people know you are acting under his authority'.

'Listen to you so bloody la-di-da'. There was a guffaw from the other soldiers and it was only then that George noticed the apprentice.

Shortly afterwards, they were fighting for their lives.

George was never really sure how it all happened. He saw the apprentice shove Ned among the clubmen. But he didn't see how the fight started from there. The clubmen were gathered behind one of the many ramshackle houses on the lane. Wearne, like most places that George had been to – although not Langport itself – had as many shacks as real stone houses. George himself had been brought up in a proper cottage made of the local blue lyas. He had been looking down on shacks like those in Wearne and he was just telling Ned this when Ned was pushed forward and into the company of a dozen scurvy looking knaves, as the sailors might call them.

Club men could be a number of things. They fought for neither side but this lot looked more like outlaws than anything else. With Ned tumbling in their midst, they grabbed their weapons quick enough. George thought they might have killed him in a second, if he'd not acted.

'Hello my good men', he made his voice go as grand as he could manage. The gentry all sounded Somerset like him but there was a bit less of it. They had to go to the King's court and talk to all sorts. He made himself sound important, to buy a second or two. The leader of the group, he supposed, swung round with a wicked looking knife raised and ready, 'I'm Sir Peter Morton and you're on my land', George told him with a little wave of his hand.

Ned had got up and was looking proper sick. George was only too aware of what this meant. He was ready to move when the other men of his troop shouted 'charge' and pushed into the mucky yard. The leader swung his knife on him but George swept it away and then smacked his fore-arm into the man's face. There was a terrible snickering noise from where Ned had been, a gurgling, a splash. The clubmen started screaming and they ran away.

George and the rest of the troop found Ned surrounded by corpses. And Ned grinning. Still grinning, he went up to the apprentice. 'You pushed me in here'.

'I saw him', George said.

The sergeant grabbed the apprentice angrily. 'What have you got against this lad?' he demanded, grabbing the apprentice by the collar. The apprentice had gone white. They watched blood draining from the dead bodies. 'Speak up, you lump of..'

'He, he hu' hurt my friend', the apprentice stammered.

'So what? You think we've time for this nonsense? I've a mind to let the lad sort you out here and now'. The apprentice started crying - large silent tears rolled down his dusty cheeks

'Come on now', the sergeant finally declared, 'We need to get back to the Aller road'. He gave the apprentice a look, pushed past him and told the young man, 'this ain't finished, don't think it is'.

He turned to George and Ned. 'You two did well — Sir David's got a good eye. You'll do well in this thing or p'raps hang. Who's to tell'. His good humour restored, the sergeant smiled and started whistling the tune 'Sally Brown'. The troop joined in with the words:

Sally Brown
Has come to town
Riding on a pony

Three times now
There's been a row
She's getting kind of lonely.

There were gales of laughter as bits of clothes or scraps of armour were passed round from the club men's bodies.

CHAPTER 4

Asleep at the Ford

❖ ❖ ❖

GEORGE FELT FUNNY ALL AFTERNOON. There was not a lot to do. He and Ned ate their lunch (bread and cheese) away from the rest of the muster. Their new sergeant – the burly sergeant had 'claimed' them – had told them to stay away from the other troops. As they showed some promise, they could be on guard duty that night. He told them to rest. They tried.

Ned straight way went to sleep. The afternoon was mild, the grass soft. George had laid his cloak down, made himself comfortable and tried to doze off. Every time he shut his eyes, he saw the dead iron sides. Or Ned's victims. Or both to-gether. He tried thinking about something else. Where they'd chased off the club men, a girl had emerged from the lean-to dairy. She'd clearly been hiding. 'That you, George Bowman', she said.

He hadn't seen her for a while. Abigail, he thought her name was. Had a sister named Hannah maybe. She'd certainly grown up. What he liked to call in his head 'a buxom wench'. Actually, he wasn't entirely sure he quite knew what that meant. In his family, it was quite god-fearing. Nobody talked about women. Even in the tavern, at the sign of the White Hart, there was not talk of girls or women. When Ned and he had worked at the wharf, he'd heard talk. They'd avoided the taverns in Langport, however, like the plague. That's what his mum had said they'd get – the plague. Watch what you drink and don't talk to the women.

He'd seen a few, though. The women. They'd shout from the doorways or from the upstairs rooms. The High Street of Langport was lined with them. Grog shops as the sailors called them. And brothels. George thought that's what they were called. You could 'hire' a girl for as much as you got paid for an hour's work! 'In and out for tuppence', one girl had shouted. Her face had haunted his dreams ever since. He wasn't wholly sure that Abigail's would take over. The girl in Wearne had given him a kiss and all the troop had jeered.

The sergeant had got rid of the apprentice. He told them, especially Ned, to leave it be. On no account was he to touch a hair on his head. The sergeant gave them his name however – John Smith, if you could believe it, called Jack – and George could not understand this either. Why tell them the man's name and stop them avenging his stupid and dangerous push.

George jerked awake with a start. He'd been back at the brawl in Wearne. Ned slept on. His hat was no longer shading his face and George moved it a little ways. Ned opened one eye, closed it and slept. The stream nearby gurgled. The bell rang at Aller church – four o'clock George thought – shut his eyes against the sun and was shaken awake in darkness.

'I must have slept', he tried to say but his mouth was full of strange dreams: Abigail firing his bow. He suddenly realised that the club man leader was most likely stunned not by his acting skills, or his sudden appearance but instead by the sight of the war bow. In the dark he reached for it now. 'No ye'll not need that now', the sergeant whispered. 'Your Ned's got a musket. Fire it if your hear sommit'. The sergeant's strange accent already sounded less strange. A bit of London in it? George had met loads of Londerners off the barges and boats at the port. They were friendly but big-headed George thought. Much like the sergeant.

He got the bow anyway. It was not yet full dark. He saw a movement in the hedgerow and shot a rabbit. It was the work of a moment, with his skinning knife, to dress it. Guts and skin lobbed further away, he found a thick stick and threaded the body down it. He felt sure that they'd be allowed a fire while they were on sentry duty. And so it proved.

It was even quite merry. The first part of the night, the sergeant shared the duty with them. He had a flagon of cider and they all shared that (the sergeant complaining about it) and the rabbit, slowly roasted over the fire so that the outer layer was quite crispy and the inside steaming hot and juicy.

'Poor man's venison', the sergeant said. He also said his name was Sam and George was not entirely sure he believed either statement. The sergeant (Sam) told a range of amusing but unlikely stories. Some of them about campaigning. Some about the supposedly huge number of women the sergeant had had. Neither George nor Ned felt like supplying stories of their own.

'Tight lipped, your friend', Sam said as he prepared to go.

'That's what my dad says too', George agreed. 'I prefer to think of him as careful. He don't know you yet. He might have to kill you'. This was stupid swagger of course but Sam was both interesting and dangerous – perhaps they meant the same thing. Sparks flew up lazily into the night and the boys listened to the night sounds, the sergeant's retreating boots. They were visited twice more.

First off, their awkward friend Nate arrived carrying apologies and pumpkin pie. George felt the former were no help but was delighted with the latter. They were a tiny bit battered from where Nate had fallen over on the short walk from his horse. 'Well, not really my horse', he muttered. 'It's really your horse. I'll pay you now, if I may'.

What sort of talk was this from another plough-boy! George thought. Actually, they were none of them really plough-boys. They could all three of them read and write, thanks to the vicar and his assistant, the mad, one-eyed Flawder. One had charmed them into book-learning and one had thrashed them into it. Although they'd failed with Billy-boy. Soon afterwards, Nate got on their horse and left, his money refused and his pies eaten

George opened a tiny book and from the light of the fire read some of Ben Jonson's words. The vicar loved the theatre. He could be side-tracked easily into tales of the Globe, of London life, the Great Freeze. The strange thing was that George had picked it up – the book and the love of this 'theatre' thing he'd never seen and might never see. It was not the same as a theatre troop arriving in Langport and staging a play on the back of a wagon.

'Ben Jonson', he said out loud, savouring the words.

'Oh God', Ned replied from the darkness, 'you're not on that again you book-worm', except he said this rude remark with several bits of swearing thrown in for good measure. They might have fought but there was a noise the far side of the fire and Ned jumped up. 'Who goes there?' he shouted. 'Friend or foe'.

Sir David stepped into the fire-light. He was somehow hard to see. 'A hot toddy?' he asked, rigging up a metal tin over the flames on a strange sort of stand. 'I'm a Jonson fanatic too', the older man declared, staring into the flames. After a while, the drink whistled on the fire. 'Mustn't let it boil', Sir David muttered, his hand taking the hot can off. The boys said nothing.

After a cup or two of hot strong liquor their voices were freed from shyness. Sir David had a way with him. ' I knew your father, Ned' he told them. And he spun some tales of battles they had fought on the continent. 'He was such a quiet, gentle man', he declared, 'until his blood got up and then he was a devil. In fact, that's what he was known as 'the English devil'. He was a terror to the Spanish and they longed to kill him but it was disease. I was there when he died'.

Ned's eyes looked longingly at their commander. It was, as usual, George that had to ask, 'would you be kind enough as to tell us about him, sir?' Ned stared, tapping at the musket stock.

'Another time perhaps', he got up and pointed into the darkness, 'here is your relief'. A few moments later, the boys heard as well. Two other men came into the firelight cursing and the two boys went to their grassy beds.

Marching Off

❖ ❖ ❖

IT WAS MID-MORNING WHEN GEORGE opened his eyes. There were sheep under the trees and grey scudding clouds. They had been allowed to sleep in for a while but the camp was all a-bustle, packing and preparing.

'Well done, you two' Sam the sergeant said, 'Sir David was impressed with you. When you've had a bite to eat, would you get the troop in marching order? Thanks'.

There was a big, steaming pot of porridge nearby and the boys stuck their bowls in and gobbled it up with their wooden spoons. As soon as they'd taken some, the company cooks took the pot away, carefully saving the remainder, to make cakes for later. In their meadow, it was fairly quiet. Over the hedge there were loud sounds – horses jingling their bridles, stamping noises and the shouts of men. They finished up, washed and drank at the stream. They went through the gate-way into a scene of complete chaos.

The 'army' was only eight hundred men. But as far as they could see, men, horses, tents were being pulled and pushed hither and thither. 'Give us a hand', a short, thick-set man demanded and they found themselves loading bales of clothing and supplies onto a wagon that was as short and squat as the man. Ned tugged at George's tunic and the two of them disappeared into the swarming mass. They found the troop at the far side of the field. 'Ready to go lads?' George asked. The apprentice was sporting a massive black eye and cradling an arm presumably bruised the same colour. It was hard to read his look but it certainly was not quite the same hatred as before.

The troop, all of them older than the boys, seemed happy to be ordered round. This was strange to George but quite a relief. It had something to do with the looks of terror, horror and admiration with which they watched Ned. With neat and tidy movements, he was bundling the weapons together – four pikes (quite a weight in itself), their few muskets and arque-busses, spare swords and cutlasses – so that each man had a load. Except them.

When Sam appeared, the troop was lined up, with the bundles shared out, ready to move. The sergeant squelched through the muddy ground, declared the work 'excellent' and shouted in a voice so loud that rooks took off from the trees, 'troop, mar-march off!'

Somehow - his shouting, the preparation - they began marching, not in time but very much together. Ned and George smiled to each other. They marched right behind the sergeant, George had his bow strung over his shoulder, the sergeant had a primed musket and Ned was as hard eyed as a hawk. There was no grumbling from the men.

At least for an hour or so. 'Fall out!' the sergeant shouted on the outskirts of Somerton and the troop dropped their bundles and lay down. Ned, George and the sergeant did not however. 'Don't take off your boots', the sergeant warned them with a snarl.

Sam, Ned and George wandered over to a cavalry detachment which was watering its horses at the stone trough. 'You've got an hour or more sergeant', the captain told him. 'I think Sir David's got a job for you a bit later'.

'Very well, sir'.

'You'll need this before nightfall' and the horseman tossed a clinking purse high in the air. Sam caught it without even looking.

'Thank ye kindly', The sergeant smiled revealing large brown teeth. He used them to pull the drawstring tight and stashed the money in his chest.

The trio came back to the troop. 'Let's learn our pikes', the sergeant shouted.

Eight at a time, they practised wheeling, retreating, advancing. However effective, George thought, the pike is the most annoying weapon. It was practically impossible not to get the twelve foot poles entangled. You dug them in, George muttered to himself, they wouldn't come out. You hold them steady, they weave all over the place. God knows.

After the twelve troopers were all sweating, cursing, exhausted over their eight poles, Sam got the cavalry troop to come and help. The horsemen charged at the pikes, only pulling up at the last minute. 'Not too bad', the captain chuckled, 'for a bunch of plough-boys'. The apprentice didn't have to do the practice because of his damaged arm. Ned, also not using a pike at that moment, wondered whether it was worth making friends. You never knew. George told him that he had to try.

So he tried.

'What happened to your arm?' he asked the man. They were both filling the troop's water bottles — a variety of containers, none absolutely leak-proof.

'As if you didn't know', was spat back.

'Obviously I don't know. What's your name anyroad?'

'Jack', the man muttered.

'Well, Jack. Whatever stupid thing you felt you had to do in Wearne, I see no need to kill you for it. Looks to me you've been punished already, though I had no part in that at all. We'm don't have to be friends but we need to stop being enemies. Shake on it?'

And they shook, Jack almost smiling from under shaggy reddish curls. 'I've no notion at all why I thought to harm you. Bloody stupid.'

'I hurt your friend – natural enough'.

'He's not even a friend. Stuck up bastard. Just 'cos his aunt owns a tannery.'

'Have an apple', Ned handed over a little wizened fruit.

'Ta, you'm a gent'. They picked up the canteens and started to trudge back. The sergeant's voice was almost hoarse from shouting and Ned noticed that George had begun to join in. 'Quick learner your friend', Jack suggested.

'He is that and all', Ned agreed, smiling at the wheeling horses and the little band of men frantically moving the awkward pikes, 'he is an' all'.

A bit later on, with the men resting, Ned picked up a pike and said to Jack, 'let me show thee summit'. He began turning the pike slowly round his head. The whole troop gathered round to watch (at a safe distance). The horses moved a little away in fear as the twirling got faster. Soon, there was just a blur. Ned spun the 20 pound pole round his arm, his neck, even round his chest. He seemed to flicker inside the whirling wood like a wraith or a will-o'-the-wisp. When he stopped, the men clapped as though this was theatre on a wagon.

When they set off marching again, they were in the best of spirits. They began to sing a song about 'Lucy the loose' which went on with dozens of verses, all the way to the Fosse Way where they put up for the night.

'Perfect marching weather', Sam said to George. 'Nice and dry, but not too dry. You don't want dust in your mouth'. The truth was that, at the front of the army, it was clean and fast and altogether pleasant.

'It's all right this is', Ned grinned at George.

'Just you wait', George thought to himself but chose not to say and spoil his friend's remarkably chatty mood.

CHAPTER 5

Caliver Men and Ragabond Music

❖ ❖ ❖

'DON'T GET USED TO IT', Sam laughed at his men, bedding down in the inn's vast stable. The army hadn't been past and the publican had actually welcomed them.

'The King's soldiers', he'd roared, 'plenty of room for you all'. He'd charged them next-to-nothing for their cider and stew and nothing at all for the bedding. 'Wenches'd come extra', he'd laughed his big fat man's laugh.

Mind you, some of the men still found something to complain about. With their boots off, their feet had swelled straight away. Some had soaked them in cold water, some had tried raising them up, like you do with a swollen ankle.

The trouble was, they all counted as volunteers. They could not really complain about being there although some of them tried to. As the youngest, George and Ned went round with the drink and food. The troop started in the main serving table, like a party. Later, when the locals found it too squashed, they were asked to move into their stable. It was safe enough, none of them could afford to smoke, and the flickering lanterns gave a soft yellow glow to the scene.

Most of the men were nodding off when Sam came round and made a gesture for them to follow him. They went into a tiny room near the bar. Sir David was already there. 'I've come to let you into our little secret'. There was a card table in front of him and onto it he placed several pieces of paper. 'I know you can both read well – I've tested it – and I want you to read these two letters'. He pushed one at each of the boys, who sat on small stools and felt like school boys. The sergeant popped out to get them another pint each (and perhaps guard the door).

'These are the papers from those two round-heads you so miraculously killed. They were scouts or spies – you must choose what to call them because I am asking you to do the same thing. I want you to check out the lie of the land, where the enemy is, what the locals are thinking.' Sir David paused.

'I think that this is in a simple code', George declared. 'If we do a straight-forward substitution, it appears to be orders addressed to Bristol, from', he took a moment to check, 'from Hampshire'.

'Very good. Now, master Ned, what do you make of yours?'

'It's a laundry list'.

'And so it is', he gave a big laugh and then abruptly stopped. 'I'll need your answer in the morning. The rest of the troop is just window dressing by the way – they have been chosen because they can march fast, no other reason. In the morning, you will be joined by three caliver men'. The boys looked at him as though he had started speaking in a foreign tongue. 'It's a small bore musket – quicker to fire and quicker to reload. They will be real soldiers. You need to think about disguises, ways to get the job done. Now, to bed!'

The sergeant roused them before dawn. The boys had spent a short time whispering to each other but fatigue had silenced them before they'd really decided. Ned muttered now to George,'let's do it' and George agreed. Fairly soon into the march and George had been able to tell the sergeant.

'This here's a Roman road', Jack had lectured the other men, before falling over and giving everyone a good laugh. Here in Somerset, they had no great need to maintain silence and, with dawn cracking the sky in the East, they began a good marching song – Mr Tolliver's relief – with all the filthy words thrown in. They soon discovered that Ned had a good rich bass voice and that George could not sing in tune at all. They continued straight as a die for four miles and then stopped for breakfast.

There was a steep hill in front of them with the roadway zig-zagging up so that horses and carts could make the climb. 'I thought them Romans made the road straight', one of the men teased Jack. Jack chuckled back. Since making his peace with Ned and George, he'd seemed much happier. Even his arm was nearly mended. He was using it now to make hot oatcakes.

Three men approached, roped over with equipment and carrying short fire-arms. They identified themselves early ('We're the culiver men – are you Sergeant Sam Gold?) but George had his bow strung and an arrow ready all the way. As they got nearer still, Ned stood with a pike ready. The other troopers were as dozy as the cow in the next door meadow, batting her big dark eyes at them and occasionally making a friendly moo. If the culiver men had chosen to attack, the troop sprawled on the verge would have had no resistance to offer.

The sergeant ('Gold', George whispered to Ned, 'what sort of name is that?') and the boys and the culiver men had met out of earshot of the rest of the troop. 'What's the password?'

'The King's Head', the oldest culiver man answered. To George they were all old – perhaps in their thirties – and nearly as old as their own parents.

'All right', the sergeant whispered, 'we have to find out about any roundheads moving around between here and Bath. These two are George' he indicated the larger boy 'and Ned' pointing at the smaller.

'Them's kids' another culiver man said with a sneer. There was a blur of movement and the man was on the ground with Ned's knife at his throat. The rest of the troop didn't even notice and the cow mooed again gently. There was a buzzing of bees. 'Jasus Christ', the man on the ground finally found his voice, 'you is fast. I won't be calling you a kid again in a horry', he chuckled and felt his neck which had been nicked by the dagger. 'Sharp knoife too', he chuckled again, even more unconvincingly. George thought that his voice sounded Irish. Some of the gypsies came from Ireland and some of the sailors at Langport.

'Right', Sam told them, 'you've sniffed each others' arses. Can we try to remember that we are meant to be on the same bloody side. 'Steeth, Ned, could you put the pig sticker away'. But George could tell that the sergeant was secretly pleased. They had done something else right. It all seemed a bit confusing – like winning a prize for something that you didn't know was happening. Also, what did they know? Perhaps all wars were fought with 16 year old spies.

As they walked up the steep hill, zig-zagging one way and then the other, the view opened behind them and they saw the Levels rolling flatly into the distance. In the distance, they could see the movements of other troops as well as the occasional herdsman and house-wife, merchant and man of business. At the top of the hill, there was half a mile of undulations with dense woodland on either side. Soft sunlight, but nippy. George's dad had told him that it'd been nippy for many years in a row.

George was the one who heard the music. 'We better check it out', George said to the sergeant. You keep going, we'll catch up'.

'All right, but take Winchpole with you' and the sergeant pointed at the oldest culiver man. The boys looked at him with doubt in their eyes but nodded.

They walked down into the dark wood, leaving the sound of the soldiers chatting loudly behind them. Even though it was a fairly bright day, not much of the light reached through the tangled woodland. Above their heads, trailed ivy and old man's beard, bramble and wild roses. The silvery notes of a flute pulled them further in. Progress was noisy – this was not managed forest, this wood had been allowed to go wild. They fought their way forward and the culiver man came behind them, carefully cradling his loaded weapon. George struggled with his bow but he'd been going through woodland to hunt since he was six. It was the culiver man who made the most noise.

A small clearing opened up and in the gloom, they could see hanging bones on string tied all the way round. In the very light wind, the bones made a tiny dry tinkling just audible under the beautiful melody. For that is what it was. Bewitching. As the thought came to George's head, he turned to look at his friend. Ned had gone white with terror. He was staring in horror at the tinkling bones but the look in his face became mad as something moved behind George.

George spun round, his bow automatically coming to hand, arrow ready strung. There was a tiny black man or woman standing above a mound of smoking sticks. Had it come out of the mound, George wondered. 'Shoot it', Ned screamed, his eyes wild and spit flecks launching from his mouth. And then Ned launched himself at the black figure, his long knife sweeping the air.

George tripped him over. The knife luckily spun away. The short figure casually put his pipe back in his mouth. The mound behind him was the same height as him. Perhaps, not so much a mound as a little black shack. Or a tiny hay stack. The music from the vagabond began again and a strange stillness filled the glade. Like magic. Ned squirmed on the ground muttering 'witches, witches'.

Shepton Mallet
and the Moon

❖ ❖ ❖

GEORGE SAT GENTLY ON NED and listened to the man talking. 'It's a lonely life', he said, warming up some milk on his perpetual fire, 'but it pays well'. He gestured to ten hessian bags of charcoal. 'That lot's worth a month's wages and it took me a week to make. My family will eat for a year for a month in the woods. What are you boys doing?'

'We're marching for the King'. Ned groaned and woke up. He opened his eyes, stared at the black man, and screamed. 'Shut up, Ned', George told him. 'It's only a charcoal burner'. That didn't seem to work. He spoke louder, 'it's a charcoal burner, A CHARCOAL BURNER'.

It amazed George how Ned could be so scared, especially of witches. He sat him up and gave him a clay cup of milk and honey. George and Winchpole had one too. And little honey cakes as well. 'I sell wild honey as well, when I can get it', the black man said. Except, of course, he wasn't really black. Even in the few minutes 'up top', as the charcoal burner described it, patches of white skin had emerged and his bright blue eyes looked like corn-flowers in a burnt stubble field. 'The farm below brings me milk, wheat and oats, and some greens'. He pointed off towards Pilltown (George thought). This side of the wood, the man had cleared the ground and there was a fine view of Glastonbury Tor, with a few patches of water, glimmering like a costly mirror.

'I need some old wood to start the burn. Then I'll coppice for a time. Mostly I want alder. Many alders. At the end, I'll need proper new oak wood. If you're careful, it'll all make charcoal. They say the price'll keep rising. You boys need your steel', he chuckled. He passed Ned's knife back to him; he took it with a smile of apology. The charcoal burner's voice had sounded all scratchy and choked at first. Now his words flowed like a tidal river rushing in. The soldiers drank their delicious drink, ate their delicious biscuits and listened to the man, sprawled like children round the village story teller. He told them things they knew already — how charcoal was used to turn pig iron into the brightest, sharpest steel. He told them things that nobody knew — riding on the moon in a shroud of silk.

The man was so hungry for human contact that he watched their faces like a hawk. He noticed Ned's look of worry. 'Them's for the wind', he tinkled a bone or two. 'I trap the rabbits, sell the skins, eat the meat and even their little bones help my business. The big danger ain't the rain. No, no, no. The big danger is a high wind. Even a little wind will stoke the fire. Right now, I need to damp it down'.

The soldiers looked around. They had not noticed any real wind but the bones rattled a bit more and the little man bustled round his mound, covering one part with wet foliage and heaping more withies on another. George noticed that there was a shimmer of heat and he felt a tiny lick of heat on his face.

'Listen, Winchpole', George turned to the culiver man, 'would you go back to the sergeant and tell him that we'll join you the other side of Shepton. I've had an idea.'

Winchpole scratched his beard and smiled. 'If he'll give me a couple more cakes, I might be able to!'

Whistling the charcoal burner's tune and cramming his mouth with honey cakes, Winchpole returned the way they'd come. George turned back to the little man. 'Listen, I might have a job for you'. The little man looked in awe at the boy. He sat down carefully.

'A job, a job' he said in a low voice. There was no question that the little man was a little odd, George thought.

But, like it or not, that was the reputation that charcoal burners had.

'I've met you before', George told him, his eyes following Ned. Ned had wondered off hunting a rabbit with his returned knife. 'With my dad'.

This seemed to turn a cog in the black man's head. He suddenly spoke sensibly. 'Yes, how is Smithy Bowman? Has his leg got better?'

'No, it ain't', George said bitterly, 'he couldn't work at all last winter. My mother had to take in washing.'

'Washing for the Bowmans of High Ham. That must have been a trial for Sir George.'

'My uncle still does not know, nor likely to find out if this war continues'.

'Why's that then?'

'Haven't you heard? My uncle has gone to join the rebels'.

'Oh me oh my', the little dark man started sorting through his faggots, snorting and spitting and muttering. His attention seemed to have moved on from the conversation. Shortly, however, he came and stood near George (too near, George thought). 'What's yon job then?'

'Well, Ezekial Kinrush, here's my idea...' He explained at length and by the time he'd finished Ned was staring at him in wonder. 'What do you think?' George asked his friend.

'I think you've finally gone completely loopy. But I like 'im. He's the sort of plan to make my blood sing. Do we have to take blackie here?'

'I don't know. Would you want to come with us?' George waited for an answer from Ezekial. It was a long time coming. Finally, he whispered, 'I could. Just the boy. You'm bin too big master George'.

And so it was settled.

By the time George had reached the big cross-roads the far side of Shepton, there was a finger nail moon in the sky and the light was beginning to fade. The troop was practising culiver manoeuvres but stopped to jeer at George.

'Where have you been?' the sergeant shouted while George was still labouring up the long hill.

'Isn't Winchpole there?'

'He is and all'. George had got near enough for fairly normal conversation but he continued very loudly still.

'Ned's been taken sick'. And then he gestured to the sergeant. 'Sam', he whispered come away here a second. Tell me off and make it look good'.

'I don't believe a word of it', the sergeant shouted and grabbed George by the ear, 'Come with me you nasty little ploughboy. I'm going to teach you some manners. The rest of you, Winchpole's in charge, get back to your exercises'. The sergeant punched George in the eye and he toppled backwards into a field bordered by high hedges.

'Ow, you bastard'. George shouted, not entirely acting.

'Teach you to call me a bastard', the sergeant roared and spun them both under the cover of the hedge, out of the way of prying eyes and prying ears.

'Sergeant I've got a plan and I want you to know nothing of it for the minute. It's like an experiment'.

'All right, we'll all act like scientists and alchemists will we?' He smiled, tousled George's head and then threw him back towards the road way.

It was full night and the moon shone high above Shepton before two figures and a donkey came slowly up the hill. The troop was lying by a big fire (no great need for conceal- ment yet, the enemy was still some way off yet, bar those two strange scouts). One of the culiver men was on sentry duty and shouted, 'stop who goes there?'

'Just two colliers', the answer came, 'can we join you at your fire? I've got honey cakes'.

Winchpole shouted, 'them's good, they are' and the men allowed the two black figures to sit and join them. The char- coal burners handed out cakes, and were given some ale in return. George took Winchpole aside and whispered some in- structions to him.

All but the sentries were soon asleep.

The Plan is Developed

❖ ❖ ❖

IN THE MORNING, GEORGE AND the sergeant were up before any-one else. They were on sentry duty together. 'What do you think?' George demanded.

'About what?' the sergeant replied.

'About them', George nodded his head towards the sleeping figures, just visible in the dawn as a series of snoring mounds.

'What about them?'

'You have no idea, do you?' George chuckled. 'I'll show you something'. He went over to the sleeping people, tapped a small black man on the shoulder and returned to the sergeant.

'That's a collier, a charcoal-burner', the sergeant said, as though George was stupid.

'No it's not', George replied. 'It's Ned'.

'Really', the sergeant stepped closer to the little black man. 'I would never have known'.

'And I wasn't even trying to fool <u>you</u>' George coughed as a wisp of the dying fire drifted into his face.

'Riders, coming this way', Ned suddenly said.

The sergeant sprang to his culiver, preparing to fire it. He shouted, 'to arms, to arms', in a voice loud enough to wake the dead and fairly successful at waking the troop. By the time a dozen horsemen crested the rise from the Bath and Bristol roads, the troop had a ragged line of pikes up and the culiver men were all ready. Sam had surrendered his culiver back to its real owner and was standing, sword drawn, in front of the troop.

'Halt in the name of the king', Sam bellowed and the riders did halt, though whether at the name of the king or the raised pikes or the smoking culivers – who knows?

'Dispatches in the name of the King', the leading horseman shouted back.

'I don't think so', George whispered, 'play for time'.

'The road's closed', Sam told the horsemen, 'You'll have to go around'. There was a shuffling and prancing among the horses. They were impatient, unnaturally so.

'Make one of them dismount', George whispered.

'I'll need to see your orders', Sam insisted and one of the riders came forward. He pretended to reach for a message in his breast but pulled out a pistol instead.

'I warned you sergeant', the man declared, before toppling from his horse with an arrow through his chest. His fire-arm discharged when it hit the dusty road and the horse took off in an eye-rolling panic, with the rider's foot still in the stirrup. The other horsemen tried to stop the grisly run-away but the horse swept through them.

'Fire', shouted the sergeant. The culivers boomed. George had six arrows in the air as, slowly, like trees falling, two of the men slid off their horses. The other nine galloped away to-wards Wells, before two more pulled up with arrows through the horses' rib-cages.

Ned, pretending to be a charcoal-burner, could make no move towards the fallen horsemen. He had to watch as George moved at half his speed and a fraction of his ferocity towards the injured. Everyone knew, everyone who had ever hunted, that the wounded are the most dangerous. A wounded wild boar would kill you in a trice. Even a wounded horse or cow would have you. Ned wanted to shout warnings. He strained against the load that had been piled upon him by his 'master', 'Mister Kinross'. He could not tell whether having to be nice to 'Mister Kinross' in public was worse than having to be in charge of him in private.

The slow-coach George had reached the first man down. Sam was shortly there as well. 'Meet us at Downside', Ned told them as the colliers passed the injured enemy. The downed man was unconscious, possibly dead. He'd come loose from the stirrup after thirty yards but even that had left a stripe of blood on the road way. The blood was rapidly turning brown and soaking into the dust.

George searched him. He had orders. From Lord Fairfax, the rebel commander, no less. The code was laughable. 'They're from Bristol. They are finding out when we be coming for them'.

'Winchpole', the sergeant shouted, 'go back to Shepton and get this message to Sir David or any other officer. Take one of these horses and join us again at', he paused and looked at George, 'Downside was it?'

It took an hour to clean up the mess. The wounded were too wounded to live. They were put out of their misery.

Everyone got something from the dead – a gold coin, a breast-plate, a dagger, half a cold chicken. Bizarrely, George was given a collection of woollen threads – enough to darn the socks of the whole company. 'Give you something useful to do', the lead culiver man told him. Everyone laughed. The two whose horses had been shot had hidden or run away.

They marched. Much more carefully. The two remaining culivers were loaded and ready. George had his bow strung and with an arrow notched. The men all had pikes 'at arms'. It made for a slow walk, hardly two miles in the hour. This was still twice as fast as the rest of the army. (They all had inch thick 'horse steaks' ready to cook in the evening. They left a trail of blood for Winchpole to follow or indeed anyone else.)

The moon was fuller that night. They made the tiny hamlet of Downside, also called Stratton, at dusk, asking at the inn – 'The Two Coins'. The publican was noticeably more nervous, did not allow them to bed down in his tavern but did sell them drink. Half the men had cider, half the men had beer.

There was a parish church and a thatched vicarage as tumble down as every other house. The vicar was drunk. 'Whas you sodgers want?' he bellowed at them but was happy enough to let them on his meadows. Sam and the sergeant went to talk in the grave-yard. Happily that's where Ned and Kinross were staying.

'First off sergeant', Ned declared, 'we need many more riders when we near the enemy. Kinross will need paying and Sir David and whoever will need to agree the plan.'

'What is the plan?' Sam enquired.

'Kinross and me'll make charcoal near the known enemy positions. When we go to get eggs or milk, we'll get messages to you. I think you'll have to tell the troop that 'Ned' has gone back home. Will we get to see Sir David any time soon?'

'That all depends', mused the sergeant. There was a cry and Winchpole arrived with a clatter of hooves. 'Quite good timing', Sam said with a smile. He passed the message to George as Ned seemed to disappear into the gathering dusk. The warm, late June air should have been warm enough but the sergeant gave a little shiver. 'Someone's walked on my grave', he thought with another shudder. The rooks called and then silence descended on the hamlet.

CHAPTER 7

The Bridge at Bradford

❖ ❖ ❖

Sɪʀ Dᴀᴠɪᴅ ʜɪᴍsᴇʟꜰ ᴀʀʀɪᴠᴇᴅ ᴀᴛ dawn. They had agreed to meet in the church yard again. The sun was barely up, a light mist, and the distant sound of men moving, snoring, farting in their sleep. Birds singing far too vigorously for how George felt. He had dreamt again of dead men - men that he'd made dead. He hoped they'd go away soon. His head ached. Ned the black boy somehow made it worse. Of course, despite everything, Sir David failed to recognise him. 'Who's this lad then?' he'd asked with the easy and entirely false good nature that he assumed with strangers.

Ned had got perfectly into the part. It worried and amused George in equal measure. He sidled up near Sir David and whispered, 'it's me, Ned Appleton'. Of course, George realised, their lives depended on this trick – Ned looking like a ten year old perhaps, slight and frail in his coating of black ash. Except for the dirt, anyone would want to comfort him, feed him up.

George was the one who had to explain the idea. 'We get Ned and Kinross near to the enemy. They can't move from where we place them for days at a time – better perhaps that they are put in place a while before they're needed'.

'By the heavens, how can I know where they'll be needed?' Despite the humour in the words, there was no humour in Sir David's voice. He might play the cheerful gentleman but, George suspected, he was neither cheerful nor gentle.

'Most of the time, they'll be travelling – locating a source of charcoal. It is only when you think there might be an engagement that you need to 'plant' them.'

'God help us all', Sir David muttered. George felt sure one of the problems was that Sir David himself had not come up with the plan.

'It was you that gave me the idea', he said, not sure why. He was neither the quickest liar nor the best. But perhaps it was true. George searched back in his memory. At that moment, the apprentice Jack stumbled over to take a piss. He never even noticed the four men huddled down behind a grave stone. He farted a long wet fart, gave a grunt of satisfaction, and went back towards the troop. 'Thank goodness he didn't need to relieve his bowels. Anyway, sir, you mentioned disguises..' George's voice trailed off. Sir David had a strange gleam in his eye.

Luckily, the older man chuckled. 'Yes, I did. Good memory George. Good initiative too'.

'Thank you sir', George muttered even though he had no idea what 'initiative' was. He realised that there was a limit to the education he'd received with the vicar.

'We'll go with your scheme but it will require a slightly different beginning. We'll send Kinross up to Landsdowne to set up his charcoal making. He'll be needed, maybe, there, in a week. You two however, I need now in Bradford on Avon. I have brought horses and some harquebusiers. It would not do for the caliver men to know that Ned was with us. I will be back with the main army advancing from Frome'.

'Why did we come on this road then sir?' George enquired politely.

'I can't get you in sideways otherwise', Sir David explained, sort of. George scratched his head. He thought he understood but like a lot of things, he did not understand completely.

That evening they looked down on the sleepy mill town of Bradford. It was swarming with Roundheads but their main force was a day or two away. How did they know that? They had asked a man bringing bundles of faggots into town. Ned was still black enough and there seemed to be some kind of secret world of wood-burners. Ned suggested that the colliers, the charcoal burners, were the kings in this world. 'Don't put on airs', George had told him and Ned looked daggers for a second then laughed, quietly.

'Looking like this I don't feel so big and clever'. He glanced around. The boys were hidden on the edge of a wood that looked down – it seemed almost vertical – into the bustling Wiltshire town. 'It's big this town though', Ned whispered and looked back again. The harquebusiers were concealed with their heavy muskets at the edge of the wood, looking out at the rolling fields. 'We've got what we came for', Ned muttered and, at that moment, there was a shout from their men and a triple crack of gunfire.

'I'm sorry', the lead musketeer apologised, 'they've seen us'. It was a disaster, George thought. Apart from the dying horse and dying man fifty yards away, all the firing had done was make a squadron of Roundhead cavalry nervous and wary. They would, without doubt, have sent for reinforcements. The boys must escape now. And tell Sir David the news. George thought fast.

'Right, you three. Saddle up and go like the wind that way', George pointed North. He and Ned slunk back into the wood, carefully steering their horses, with a hand over their muzzles, away from the enemy. Even if they weren't spotted, they had a hell of a job on. George thought and thought of some clever plan but nothing better came to him.

A hundred yards west, the boys mounted up as quietly as they could. There had been some shouting and gunfire a few moments before. George hoped that the harquebusiers would not be killed but he'd no choice but to use them as a lure. It was all a bit like hunting, although right now it was him and Ned that were the plump partridges waiting to fall into the snare, the rabbits that must run.

And run they did, crashing out of the edge of the wood into a flat out gallop, straight up a slight hill and round another stand of trees, then stopping on a sixpence. The horses were superb, George patted his, a dark grey and looked at Ned's, a light bay. They would be well nigh invisible in the evening twilight, both as grey as the light. There was no sound, no pursuit. However, they had no time to lose but must still take especial care. Walking and trotting, they made their way south, keeping well away from Bradford and its historic bridge.

They slept in a wood again. They were getting used to it. Their saddlebags were full of (fairly stale) bread and some unidentifiable dry-ish meat (horse?). There was a stream. It was as dark as the pit of hell and, rightly or wrongly, George decided they needed sleep more than a sentry.

Later, George thought, as sleep stole upon him, we might get used to riding without a moon. That night he dreamt of his mother's apple pie and of his father, miraculously uninjured.

When he looked out of the cottage window, in his dream, the sky was the colour of blood.

They woke to the wood full of mist. They made their way south, every noise dampened by the weather and beads of moisture forming on their wool and running down their leather. They were in the middle of a cavalry patrol before they had even noticed. Swords were drawn and pistols cocked before George could get his bow off his back.

'Who are you?' the cavalry leader shouted hoarsely. The horses neighed horsily. George was struck dumb and Ned had to answer.

'We're with Sir David'.

'You should have said', the leader drawled casually. 'Jenkins, find Sir David right now. These are the', he paused and eyed the boys, 'men he was expecting'. There was a clatter as trooper Jenkins found the road and galloped away. 'Timpson, a fire, a hot drink, some food for these', the man paused again, 'boyos'. There was, in his accent, suddenly a hint of Welsh.

George and Ned got off their horses and fell over.

CHAPTER 8

A Bridge (The Short Version)

❖ ❖ ❖

DESPITE BEING SO SHORT OF time, it took ages to work out a plan. George had started reporting so fast, 'and then we were chased and I sent the musketeers over to the other copse and I think that they were all killed or captured..' that Sir David had laughed a surprisingly full-bellied guffaw.

'Ho ho ho', is what it sounded like. 'Take it easy. We can't understand a word you are saying'. With Sir David was another man who kept in the shadows but could not stop himself striding around. He too uttered strange barks of laughter.

An hour into the meeting (they all had glasses of wine in real glasses) and they had hardly started. 'You think we could force the bridge do you lads?' George said yes and Ned nodded. 'Explain to us what you think that would involve'. They were in a tent so enormous that it was bigger than most houses. Real furniture sat on real Persian carpets. It was all so real, why did it feel like a dream to George?

George used a scrap of paper and drew the bridge, as they had seen it – from above and from the North. He sketched in the Saxon church and gave an indication of the woollen mills that had made the town very rich. It was the great wealth that had allowed the beautiful three arched bridge to be built. 'What I was thinking was this', he gestured at the road that led to the bridge, 'a very quick group of horsemen could rush into the town and take the South end while Ned and I and some other sneaky men could approach the North end'. Sir David looked at him with approval and made approving noises.

The man in the shadows also became too interested and approached the drawing. George saw who it was and bowed deeply, 'your highness', he declared, dragging Ned with him so that the smaller boy seemed to bow as well. Prince Rupert waved away this formality.

'Ve have met before, yes George? You can call me 'sir'. Ve are friends, ja?' and again the barks of laughter. 'Now, ze plan. Vy not take a horse and cart and stop it at ze far end of ze bridge. You and you troops can emerge and hold off any nosy guards while my cavalry storm the other end'.

'How will you know when to come, sir?' George enquired.

'Good question...' he thought for a while and turned to Sir David, who had been watching the planning with a cold smile on his face.

'Could they send up a rocket?' Sir David apparently didn't need to say 'sir'. That impressed George a great deal. He took another sip of wine. He had not had the drink often before and he wasn't sure he liked it. It seemed thick, like drinking blood.

Ned suddenly chimed in, 'what if we have an 'accident' with the cart? What if it becomes tangled up at the far end so that the guards cannot be reinforced?'

'It vill be a sticky ten minutes, huh? Who shall go vith zese boys, David? You are too old I zink?' and he laughed again.

'Shall we have men hidden in the cart?' Sir David asked George.

'I 'spose so', George had not considered how the storming of the bridge would develop.

'Are we the right people to do this?' Ned asked.

Everyone turned to look at the smaller boy. Sir David got a look in his eye. 'Look, you two. One minute are plough-boy volunteers and the next you are in council with me and Prince Rupert. There never has been a faster promotion. However, if you are to spy for me, you have to continue to look and act like the thickest yokels. Oo ar, Zummerzet zider', he suddenly broke into broad Somerset and Ned giggled loudly. George suddenly realised that his friend was drunk. The wine was strong. 'I do not want to lose you', Sir David continued, 'my pretty plough-boys and I won't. The thing has to be planned perfectly and it's worth risking you. It is the other men with you who will die – just like the musketeers we lost to get this information. They will be the very best men and I will sacrifice them for the bridge'.

George was fairly sure that Sir David had entirely failed to answer the question. George wondered what they had got themselves into. He felt surprisingly calm, but that might have been the wine. There was nothing they could do about it. They went out of the tent, staggering slightly, to see about the preparations for the morrow.

They needed a cart with a horse. Ned came up with the excellent idea of filling it with faggots – bundles of wood that were essential to the charcoal burner's art but also useful to every household – bread ovens all were 'fired' with faggots. They practised hiding people under the faggots and it was possible but fairly uncomfortable. There wasn't time to make special hiding places but Ned also suggested using firewood blocks to help protect the soldiers hidden under the load. This seemed to work quite well.

It was night-fall before Sir David brought the soldiers. Ned and George were hiding in an orchard on the South side of the town. They had their horse and cart, with its load. Ned had struck up a strong relationship with their pony, a cob of a variety of colours and called by George a 'gypsy beast'.

'Right you two, what've you bin up to?' a familiar voice asked. They knew who it was, even in the dark.

'Sergeant Sam', George bellowed and gave the old cockney a buffeting hug, 'we are so glad to see you'. Even the silent Ned seemed to agree. There was a quiet noise of agreement.

'Couldn't let you do this on your own. Seems like there was a bit of dodgy business needing an old hand'.

'Telling me', George agreed. 'Have you been told the plan?'

'Yeh', Sam pulled out a jug of cider, 'I've brought you this. We'll drink your apple muck while you explain it all to me', he paused briefly, 'and to these lot – they are my old muckers'.

George felt he had never seen such a villainous mob. Each of them brought out a flagon of cider and, in the firelight, their faces flickered and smiled like a demon host. Hardly a one had many teeth left. Every one was missing some part of their face or body – an eye here, fingers, a hand, several ears.

'If you're the good soldiers, what do the bad ones look like?' Ned, amazed, asked. George stared open mouthed at his friend. What had made him speak? And why something so aggressive with these battle-scarred monsters of men? There was a low growl, like wolves in the distance as George's dad had described it. Then a pause, as though hell was about to break loose. Finally, as George put his hand on his sword, a great gushing roar of laughter.

'You were right, Sam', a Scottish voice muttered between guffaws, 'these are the right lads all right'.

'Talk in English you Scottish bastard', another voice, surprisingly high-pitched, declared. There was the sound of a huge blow and the thud of someone falling on the orchard grass.

'Understand me noo, ye sasannack cromb' the Scottish voice laughed again and, again after a bit of a wait, the high-pitched voice joined in. George wondered to himself what they had got themselves into. The 'real' soldiers seemed even more unlikely to force the bridge than him and Ned on their own. Well, at least Sam was here.

They did not sleep much that night.

CHAPTER 9

Storming the Avon

❖ ❖ ❖

GEORGE WOKE, AMAZED THAT HE'D slept at all. Bits of him hurt
and his head throbbed. Why had he gone out drinking with
Sam? He could hardly remember the night's adventures. He
found an old coin round his neck, on a leather thong. He wondered for a while where that had come from and then he remembered. Even on his own, alone in the orchard, he blushed
and with the blush came a smile and a sudden boiling of animal
energy in his blood. He jumped up and threw Ned's blankets
off him. Ned swore at him sleepily, not concerned with his
own nakedness. He also had a medal round his neck. The sight
made George pause. He went outside to get them some breakfast porridge.

Their group of soldiers were all stirring, dotted round
the orchard like piles of rubbish. George scanned the sky. It
was July but it was not going to be hot, he decided. Like every country person (which meant almost everyone on earth),
George could tell pretty much what the weather was going to

be like. He could smell a bit of rain in the air. All to the good. He was carrying two bowls, swimming with fresh cream when Sir David sidled up, pulling the boys into the tent with him.

'Let's go through the plan once more', Sir David told them. The boys slurped down their food, one then the other detailing the complicated operation they had cooked up. 'All right', Sir David smiled quickly, 'load up the cart. I will get everyone else away from here.'

Not many minutes later, anyone watching would have seen two boys taking a load of firewood North. And there were people watching. Thousands and thousands of people. George had never seen so many people and he did not have to act in order to stare in amazement. Every square inch of grass had soldiers, sitting, eating, organising their equipment. There were mini-blacksmitheries, mobile bakeries, horse doctors and surgeons. The eyes of their own army watched them leave. Even more amazing, Prince Rupert gave a barely perceptible nod to them, in the middle of shouting loud, German-accented orders.

Their wooden wheels rumbled on the hard-packed, and sometimes, paved, roadway. They were soon sweating, despite the mild weather. Driving a pair of mules was very hard work but making this cob move was the very devil. George tugged at his collar, Ned swished a whip. It was part of the act. Sir David had made that very clear. They were acting. Every moment.

Hot and flustered, they had left the thousands of Royalists behind. They came over a slight rise and there were the spewing chimneys of Bradford-on-Avon. On the road was a simple log across the road and two Roundhead sentries. The boys hardly looked at them. In fact, the taller man had to shout (a cockney voice a bit like Sam's), 'oi, you two bloody plough-boys. Where d'ya think you two are going? The road's closed you bloody yokels', except there were five more swear words. The shouting brought an officer out to the barrier.

It was Ned that shouted to the man, ''tis your ironmaster wants this wood'. The officer was a local. He squinted at the boys.

'Where are ye from?' George could tell that this was a Wiltshire man asking. The accent was a little less sing-songy than theirs. A bit flatter. He looked friendly though – no point lying.

'We'm from Somerset. Somerton originally but Frome recently'. George suddenly worried that the words were too long, too educated but he needn't have worried. The officer waved them through and, between them, they got the useless cob moving again. 'Gypsy horse, gypsy horse', George found himself repeating Ned's curses, as he rhythmically slapped the multi-coloured rump.

The boys hardly had a moment to gawp at the grand houses. Like everywhere else they'd ever been, the outskirts of
the town were a jumbled mass of daub and wattle (effectively
just mud clinging to thin bits of wood) with the roofs many
different colours of thatch. There were hundreds of funny
lean-tos and shacks and grubby children came out to stare at
them, clutching dolls made of blocks of wood or accompa-
nied by mangy curs that barked. Gradually, they passed the
poor people. The houses began to drag themselves higher.
They started to dress themselves in stone with stone tiling
on the roof. They passed the houses of prosperous merchants
all abustle with servants and washing. The smell changed.
Where it had been shit and muck, now it was lavender and
fragrant apple wood smoke.

They passed a small market. The noise of competing hawk-
ers rolled past the boys as they rolled past the stalls. And then,
finally, there were shops. Ned and George stared in astonish-
ment. Langport had shops but nothing like these.

The most amazing thing of all was the writing on the sign-
boards. 'William Davis, Haberdasher'. 'Isaac Treakle, chan-
dler'. 'Paull and daughters, millinery'. The shops served people
who could read. People who lived in stone houses. Of course,
Ned and George could read. Also, as it happened, they lived in
stone houses. But the part they were playing required them to
be the lowliest of farm-hands. And, luckily, the cob made their
role all too obvious and real. They slowly progressed through

the town, pulling and pushing the useless brute. Each was afforded glimpses into the houses of the rich merchants. Standing up in the cart, George could see starched white-clothed servants, bee hives, washing drying on box trees, even the occasional carp pond, drifting slowly past like a particularly good dream.

Apart from a few town's folk, the road was dotted with soldiers. Enemy soldiers. As they approached the bridge itself, the groups of soldiers became thicker and thicker. The sentry at the near side stopped them. 'Your business', he said curtly.

'We'm bringing firewood to your iron-master'. The story had worked once, why not give it another go?

'His name and your authorisation?'

George didn't need to act. His mouth swung open, 'Wha'? Oi've no papers and I don't know your ironmaster's name'.

For some reason, the answer satisfied the sentry. He walked round the cart once more and nodded them through. The wooden wheels rumbled on the stone bridge. Sea gulls cawed overhead. There was a smell from the river. The water looked filthy – all the mills dumped their rubbish, and the town's folk. 'Smells eh?', Ned asked smiling. Underneath the smile, George could see another, different smile. Ned loved a fight and he was getting ready for it.

The other side of the bridge was a very different story. The sentry was very old indeed – perhaps thirty five – with steely eyes and steely hair. He gave them the longest of looks. Ned stood by the horse's head and tried to 'calm' the animal. Really, he made him misbehave more, dragging the cart one way and then the other. The wheels made a terrible squeaking on the cobbles which hardly improved the old sentry's mood. 'Shut your fearful din!' he shouted and prodded and poked round the cart. He didn't seem to like what he saw. Finally, as if at random, he picked up the rocket. 'And what the hell's this?', he demanded.

'I'll show you', said George and their horse made wilder and wilder turning motions. George could see the left side wagon wheel wobble. The sentry was distracted. George got out his tinder box and lit the fuse. By the time the sentry turned round the rocket was hissing and fizzing. George stuck it into the top of the cart and punched the sentry in the gut. He doubled over and George kneed him in the face. The rocket shot off in a shower of sparks and the wagon wheel fell off, slewing the cart round and blocking much of the road. Above their heads, the rocket exploded in a welter of fire. The wood and soldiers slid out of the cart and George pulled out his concealed pike. It was slightly shorter than the ones that they had made.

Perhaps that is what got Ned shot.

Before that happened there was a jumble of events. And, most of all, Ned held off ten or twelve roundhead troopers with his pike. Sam was the first soldier to recover and he got some muskets ready behind the cart. George and Ned, for all the fancy talk, faced a dozen or so bridge guards on their own. George got his sword from the cart.

The enemy shouted as they ran. George could not really hear the words – perhaps 'alarm alarm' and 'the enemy' – but a confused hubbub. The rocket was still falling slowly from the sky as the boys confronted this screaming mass of soldiers. George parried two sword thrusts and then Ned was whirling. He caught two of the enemy troopers on the head and they fell unmoving. The rest backed off. George could see one of them fumbling with a pistol but Ned had also seen him. The pike, however, was that bit shorter and the man was able to sway out of the way, raise the gun and shoot Ned. Ned's eyes went wide with surprise and he was bundled backwards under the cart by the impact. 'Ned, Ned' George shouted, parrying again and again. Then there was the roar of muskets and George's assailants were swept away like dolls.

CHAPTER 10

Fiercely Bowman

❖ ❖ ❖

GEORGE HAD TIME TO GLANCE at his friend – eyes closed, tongue lolling pinkly against his still-black skin – before he grabbed his bow. He'd organised for the six foot yew to be placed just under the lip at the front of the cart. His quiver of arrows was just beneath it. George was strung in a second and, with a cold efficiency, a murderous rage in his heart, he started killing people. His back was to the bridge and to the cart under which Ned's body lay. He fired at the approaching enemy, hardly aiming, spraying the narrow road. He shot the entire quiver of twenty four arrows in under five minutes. The Prince's cavalry appeared, rattling over the bridge, each horseman had a musketeer standing on a stirrup and they dropped the gunmen off before continuing their hunting through the North end of the town.

Not far behind them were running soldiers. They killed the sentries on the South side and came round to relieve the bridge-stormers. Only when everything was secure did George stop killing. The musketeers gave him an odd look, which he didn't see. He was down on his knees under the cart, even while there was shouting and firing around him. The parliamentarians were trying very hard to withdraw, as fast as they could.

Ned looked peaceful. There was a small quantity of blood on his chest, like the amount from a nose bleed. George reached forward to close his friend's mouth. He thought death should at least be dignified. Ned's mouth was still warm! George felt for his pulse. There was one! Strangely, that was when the tears came. Once he started sobbing, he seemed he couldn't stop. Sam had to pull him out from under the cart. 'Don't worry lad – that's how it takes some people'.

'No, no, n-no', George jabbered, 'Ned's alive!'

'What? I saw him get shot'. Sam scratched his head, 'are you sure? You're not just making it up?' Sam crawled under the cart and checked on Ned. He emerged holding a strangely-shaped object on a piece of leather. 'What's this?' he demanded. George took the object from him and prized out a pistol bullet wrapped in a old silver disc. 'Worked like a charm, eh?' and, with tears in his eyes still, George found himself laughing along with Sam and, just as before, unable to stop.

'What's so bloody funny?' a quiet voice said behind him. Ned had crawled out, his face startling white where it wasn't black. He rubbed at his chest, examining the little hole. 'A bit bloody lucky', Ned declared before passing out again. Someone came past with two bottles of brandy and handed one to Sam. Their oddly assorted musketeers came back too – all clutching bottles. Right there, on the cobbles at the North end of the bridge, they started drinking. They managed to force some brandy down Ned's throat as well.

George had to go and check Ned every few minutes, to check he was still alive. Soon they were all singing – 'green grow the rushes oh' and 'the cider drinker'. They had to teach Sam who had his own drinking songs like 'oranges and lemons'. Soldiers moved past them, the cart was removed and they drifted gradually (keeping the unconscious Ned with them like a pet) to the side of the road. Propped up against a very grand merchant's house, they watched the industrious and busy townsfolk tidying the bodies. There weren't that many. Perhaps forty all told, George thought, belching. He decided that he must stop drinking.

Sir David swam strangely in front of him. 'Right lad', he said sternly, 'you and your pal need to come with me. Do you need help?' George tried to stand and, after a couple of failed attempts, did uncertainly gain his two feet. He looked down at Ned.

'I can't carry him, surrr'. Strangely, with drunkenness came the thickest yokel accent ever. George laughed to himself. Sam appeared, entirely free of any sign of drunkenness, despite having polished off a bottle of brandy on his own.

'I'll bring him, sir', he declared. He magicked up a handcart and loaded the snoring Ned with surprising gentleness. They set off, back over the bridge, standing aside as further foot-soldiers marched over, messengers and officers pushed through rudely until they saw Sir David and then they went very quiet.

All the signs of the skirmish had disappeared, the day had advanced. George felt, as he carefully made his way, stepping with too much care and watching, surprised, as his feet continued to carry him, that hours had passed without him noticing. 'Hang on a second', he declared and plunged his head into a horse trough near the market that they'd come past earlier. The market was still going. A man was shaking out an awning with 'G. Du Pont' written on it and a wheel barrow with small box trees creaked its way over towards them. George checked on Ned.

They continued, away from the enemy and back, eventually, to the orchard and Prince Rupert.

'Vell, the Prince declared, waving his glass of red wine. They all had a glass, although Ned's was full of milk and George was worried that his would make him sick. 'Vell', the Prince repeated, 'a bluddy good job you fellows did too'. There was a pause while everyone tried to understand the Prince's words. George was quickest and gave his thanks modestly. It was all he could do not to throw up on the cavalry commander.

'I vant to tell you vat ve are doing now. Is zat all right with you Sir David?'

'Whatever you fancy, your highness'.

'Goot, goot. Ve are chasing the enemy up towards Bath. Ve expect to bring them to battle in a matter of a few days, a veek at the outside. Your job will be to spy on their movements'. He moved towards a map, set up on a folding table. George spent the minutes staring unseeing at the table. He controlled his breathing. Breathe in, try not to be sick. Breathe out, try not to be sick. When they were allowed to leave, George sprinted away, vomited behind a tree, turned round, knelt down and passed out. He had confused dreams of Bradford High Street and the girl who had given him the charm.

He woke in a sweat. He was covered in a sheepskin but it was his nightmare had woken him. It was not all the people he had killed. He made his peace with that in the dream. Well, he made his peace with the dead. They had come forward, one by one, and he had shaken their hands, some hands bloody from the arrow wounds. Most still had the arrow or arrows in them, necks, chests, eyes, guts. They left him and faded away.

What had woken George was not being able to find Ned. 'Where is he, where is Ned?' he shouted in the dream and when he jolted awake the question was still hot on his lips. 'Ned', he whispered and soon found him, curled up, nearby. He had a bandage showing white on his chest. It was moving towards dawn. There were soldiers awake, quieting horses while they were readied. Carts and wagons were being loaded, the shaft propped up on blocks of wood so that the horses could be put in harness without tipping the load. It was not, George knew, the best way of doing it but everyone must be in a tearing hurry.

His mouth felt dirty. He tried rinsing it out. Someone gave him a leather bottle of 'fresh water'. George drank deeply. Then with considerable care, he knelt down and threw it all up again.

'Better out than in', Sam declared, slapping him on the back.

'And what makes you so bloody cheerful' George asked weakly, a thin dribble on his chin. He rubbed his whiskers. He did not have to shave often but he felt he needed a shave now.

Sam said, 'ta da' and brought out a steaming pot of water and a razor. 'You sit here', he ordered, hoiking over a stool with his foot. 'I'll show you why I was the best shaver in all of London town'. George allowed himself to relax as the keen blade took away his sixteen year old's 'beard'. Sam was kind enough to make no remark about the quantity or otherwise of stubble. At the end, Sam sighed like an artist finishing a painting. 'Go and relieve yourself. That's the army way. Wash, shave and the latrines. Makes you feel like a new man. We have work to do in front of the army'.

CHAPTER 11

Getting Ahead

❖ ❖ ❖

'IF YOU WANT TO GET ahead, get a horse', Sam declared patting his sorrel mare on her broad rump. George did not answer. The movement made him somewhat queasy. Not too bad but no room for idle chit-chat. Ned was never keen on chit-chat and George knew that his wound hurt him. Over the roughest ground, he took sudden sharp intakes of breath, as though surprised each time. George wondered which bits hurt but he was concentrating so very hard on not being sick, he had nothing left to ask with. No breath. No energy.

And to make it worse, the normally quiet and sensible Sam was as bubbly as a love-struck laundry-maid. George had noticed nothing of where they'd been. He had noticed the moment that they'd over-taken the front guard of the army. The men of the vanguard had watched in silence as the sergeant and the two boys trotted past. In fact, a small group of cavalry had gone with them. George thought that perhaps they were whispering about them. An army is the worst gossip factory in the world, Sam had told him while shaving him. The name of

'George Bowman' was on everybody's lips, Sam had told him. There had been a warning in that, he thought. His dad would be proud of him but no use doing what they were doing if they became famous. Fame was a kind of death. So, as soon as they left their escort, the three of them had stopped and changed their appearance. Ned had 'blacked up' again.

They passed few people in a landscape streaked with rain. The horses' hooves, even at a walk, sunk holes in the verge, whenever they over-took a stray cart. Nobody gave them a second glance. They stayed the night at Compton Basset, only a short day's ride from Bath. The inn-keeper seemed uninterested in them, his daughter less so. She finally succeeded in taking Sam off with her and the boys laughed, half envious and half relieved.

The next day was brighter. By mid-afternoon they had spotted the copse upon which they had agreed. They had ridden up the steep hill of Landsdowne and the city of Bath spread itself below them. 'Not so very big really', Ned had muttered.

'Wait 'til you see London!' Sam declared and George wondered why they would ever see London, or the New Year for that matter. The smoke from a hundred fire-places laced the air. And this was summer. George imagined that winters were hard to breathe. Coal, some of it, he guessed. That was the new-fangled fuel. Used to be that coal was picked up on the sea shore, down in Dorset and elsewhere too – sea coal it were called, he said silently to himself. Now, he thought, it might come by boat from Lancashire, maybe to Bristol. The pale sun lit the rooves and their horses' hooves moved impatiently.

'Lots of thatch in Bath', Ned muttered to himself. They walked away, still silent. What the sight of Bath had brought home, George didn't know but it all seemed less of an adventure, suddenly. A flea bit him and he yelped, scratching and caught it in his finger-nail.

'Got you, you little bastard', he said gleefully and the others laughed, as though what he'd said was funny, which it wasn't. He realised that it was his mood that was depressing them, making Sam act silly and Ned even quieter. He made an effort. 'What did you agree on, then, Ned me lad?'

Ned almost smiled in relief. 'We all ride into the copse and wait. He'll find us. He doesn't want us searching every which way for him'.

It was the mass of people, George realised. Bath was sobering because all those people lived there – thousands. And the enemy was there as well, of course. The Royalists had spent a fortune on defending the city and then simply opened the gates. That, more than anything, had got people's blood up. A bit of Somerset surrendering. It was an affront, an insult, a slap in the face. People had flocked to the colours in droves. It had ended up being a huge boost to the Royalist cause. 'Remember Bath' the news-sheets had read.

It was later in the afternoon that they found Easy Kinross, or more exactly, Easy found them. Ned had taken them by a circular route into a circular piece of woodland on the top of Landsdowne. The horses were puffed out by the climb up the long, steep hill and they ambled along the plain on the top. The right copse was about an acre of woodland - not nearly enough for the charcoal burner - quite near the long hill. When the horses had entered the woodland, they had stopped. The brightness outside was replaced by a soft gloom and the hiss and rattle of mosquitoes. They could not stop themselves from slapping at the pesky insects and Easy appeared, dark and small, before they saw which way he had come.

'Don't think much of your arriving in secret', he laughed. 'I heard you over the other side of the wood'.

'What have you bin doin'?' Sam asked, looking in disgust at the charcoal burner's arms, covered in blood up to the elbow.

'I 've bin makin' our supper', he said with some dignity. 'It is rabbit stew a la Easy'. Ezekial sat down on a tree root and started wiping off the blood with handfulls of grass. 'Also, and notwithstanding, I have made my next charcoal clamp. It is right here', he swept aside a few branches of elder, still holding on to a few snatches of elderflowers, and there in another small clearing was the strange construction by which Easy made a difficult living. There were already strange heat glimmers coming off it and Easy went over to it 'to feel your heat' as he muttered out loud to it.

'I'll leave 'e', Sam said and moments later he had. They listened to him cantering away.

The boys stood near the charcoal clamp. Even though fairly new, it was already entirely blackened. Easy's voice came from inside the 'door', 'I'll be needing a load of alder. This 'ere copse ain't big enough for a smidgen of a burn'.

'You do know we are here to find out about the enemy', George said with some bitterness. The smell of the rabbit stew was making his stomach roll over and over like a small boy rolling down a steep hill. In fact, the thought of a small boy rolling down a hill made George feel even dizzier. He sat down on a log.

Easy looked confused and scratched his head. 'Oh yes, so you are. George Bowman, isn't it? ha ha', he laughed for no apparent reason and stirred the stew. He had added cubes of rabbit (George had tried hard not to look) and was adding sorrel and horse-radish. 'I like her quoite hot', he muttered to himself and then remembered that he was having an actual conversation with real humans, 'yes, George Bowman, you need to get me the timber so that I can make the charcoal. That is your 'cover story'. You look for the wood and you watch the enemy'. He went back to muttering to himself. 'Go to the farm to the North', he finally shouted from the 'door', 'and come back for your stew in a nhour and an 'alf'.

It seemed odd to be setting off at dusk in order to see what the enemy was doing. In fact, George thought, it made them look suspicious and furtive, although they were not the words that he used in his head. 'Don't look lairy now!' he told Ned. 'In actual fact, we'm ought to be singing'.

'Singing?' Ned whispered, appalled. He was all for sneaking around silently in the dark.

'Off we go', George declared, 'Green grow the rushes oh', he began, his good humour returning. Very reluctantly, Ned joined in, his clear baritone ringing in the dusk. They went north, a garish sunset to their left, falling off Bristol way and sinking into the sea that was like a thin line of gold on the horizon. They stopped their horses to watch the sun kiss the sea, not breaking their song.

'I'll give ye six oh, green grow the rushes oh' and then trotted on again in tune (for a change). Perhaps it wasn't the sea at all, George mused to himself. Perhaps it was something else - a river. He knew that the Bristol Channel was that way but he'd never actually been here before, so what did he know? It was *terra incognito*, as the vicar liked to call it, when he was teaching them his maps.

In a few moments they espied a light and joined a clear track that led down into the warm and welcoming lights of a farmhouse. They skirted a large wood that followed the folds in the ground, down from the huge plain of Landsdowne. The lights grew nearer as they plodded onwards; George's mood changed as utterly as the night follows the day. It got darker - he felt lighter.

CHAPTER 12

The Farmhouse in the Dark

❖ ❖ ❖

THE OUTSIDE OF THE FARMHOUSE was ablaze with light but it was the farmyard that was abuzz with people. A strident voice that George thought was perhaps a child's was ordering around a large number of farm labourers.

'Finish loading the wagon', the voice insisted, 'and then harness the horses'. There was a large load of wood - hard to see how more could be fitted on top - and two men holding the halters of the largest, fattest shire horses that the boys had ever seen. They'd need to be strong taking that load, George thought.

'Halloo, halloo', he shouted to get someone's attention.

'You Easy's boys?' the bossy voice asked and into the light from a collection of lant-horns, there stepped what? George's mind went sort of blank. He couldn't really grasp it. The sight. A girl. In white. Smiling in the light. A radiance in the night. Quite.

Ned was not affected and, in the unusual event of George's silence, was forced to talk. 'Yes ma'am', Ned said, his voice as usual hardly there at all. George was still struck dumb. His horse skittered on the cobbles, slightly spooked by the lack of movement from its rider.

She stood for a moment, arms akimbo. She seemed a little puzzled by them too. She swept a strand of brown hair from her face, shrugged and said 'Come and have a mug of ale!', setting off towards the farmhouse and shouting a last few orders over her shoulder. 'Diamond and Peter, you can hitch up the draught horses now! Bring the load to the front.'

'Between a rock and a hard place', George said and blushed in the dark at his own idiocy. Why say something so stupid? And hadn't his voice sounded funny?

There was a gruff bark, a laugh ('phew' thought George) and then 'Easy old us you were sharp 'uns And us, before you ask, is me and my dad. This is he, Sir William Weston'. There was a figure hunched over in the doorway who lifted another lant-horn and showed a smiling mouth and twinkling eyes, grey hair. 'These are Easy's boys', she spoke in a gentler voice, 'come to have some ale with us, father'.

'Oh, good good', the figure said, retreating into house, 'come into the parlour'.

The parlour was a large room with high-backed settles on three sides and a long refectory table down the middle. At the end away from the window, there was a stone fire-place and above it a smallish painting of a woman. The two sconces either side shone a clear light onto her face.

'It's the Mona Lisa', George said, entranced. He'd heard tell of the painting from the vicar - even been lucky enough to see an etching. But that gave away nothing of the strange, almost magical beauty of the oil painting.

'Yes, it's a copy of course. I saw the real thing in Florence, in my travels. I had Fra Pantillo make me a copy. Not quite as good as the real thing but all we'll get in this god-forsaken England'. He coughed sharply.

'Father, calm yourself', the girl settled him down in an armchair, placed his stick beside him and gave him a mug of ale. George saw that he had a bad leg. He spent a moment rubbing at it, a movement that had become a habit perhaps.

George gratefully took his own mug and the girl smiled down at him, 'I'm Catharine Weston. In the absence of my brothers, I'm running this farm'. George stammered his thanks, looking at his feet so that he could better remember her face. He gave it another glance and she caught his look, even as she served Ned.

'I'm George and this is Ned'. There was something in the situation that made him lessen the Somerset in his voice. After all, his father Smithy Bowman had once been a gentleman. He did not, however, offer her a surname. They were spies after all.

George supped his ale and tried to sum up what she looked like. He had real trouble. Simple adjectives ('lovely'/ 'beautiful'/ 'pretty') didn't seem to help. She had sparkly eyes? Sparkly dark eyes? Hair the colour of ripe corn? He looked at her and he could find no words. He looked away and he had nothing. The moment stretched and time passed but George did not know how long. It was full dark outside. The farmhouse in the dark. Catharine in the dark.

His mug was empty and there was a sudden clattering outside. Stamping. Shouts. The rattle of bridles and something else. The rattle of weapons. Also more shouting and the tread of people through the front door. George stood and, he knew not why, moved to the gloom behind the largest of the three settles.

The soldiers who burst into the room brought a complicated mixture of smell (horses), sights (a sort of uniformish) and noises (more rattles and bangs). They also brought a very tall but painfully thin officer with a loud, high-pitched voice. 'I am the Colonel commanding the Bath area and, most especially, the Landsdowne plain. As such, you are under military orders that require that I or my men know the movements of the land-owners, their servants and attendant personages'.

George lowered his head and shut his eyes. The voice, grating and deeply annoying was not one that he had heard for ten years. However, once heard and never forgotten. 'My uncle', George muttered to himself and felt Catharine's eyes upon him. He moved deeper into the shadows.

Catharine's father was talking 'I am Sir William Weston and would expect some measure of courtesy from your troops'.

'I know who you are, Sir William, better than you might imagine'. There was a thin smile on his thin lips. 'My name is Colonel Sir William Bowman and my men and I will furnish exactly the level of courtesy that you deserve and require. I will be requisitioning the wagon and the load of wood outside'.

'I think not, Sir William', declared Sir William, 'the wood is for a charcoal burner. Charcoal burners must be afforded every help, according to your standing orders. Here are his lads come to take the wood away'. And so it was that Sir William Bowman's cross and razor-sharp attention came to be directed at Ned and George.

Not for the first time, Ned overcame whatever resistance he had to speaking and putting himself in the spotlight. He knew that this was George's uncle. 'Ned Appleton, zur', he spoke in the thickest Somerset accent imaginable. 'We'm come from master Ezekial gather this load o' wood'.

Sir William Bowman eyed him with the most complete disgust. He turned away in horror at a plough-boy, a yokel, a small grubby little tyke and strode out of the farmhouse without another word. George breathed easier.

There was a short pause and then they all went to sit down again. Ned stopped George by the settle. 'Now we'll have to kill them', he whispered.

'What?' George gasped, 'Are you mad? You are out of your mind'.

'All right', Ned muttered, no sign of any emotion on his face, 'what's your solution? They know who you are'.

'But they don't know that we are working for the king'.

They all sat down again. Catharine stared intently at George. 'Are you working for the king?' she demanded. The boys stared at each other confused. How could they answer this? 'I was asking because we are working for the royalists'.

Her father interrupted. 'As an English soldier, I took an oath. Nothing that has happened, in parliament or elsewhere, absolves me from that oath. I simply do not understand how soldiers that have served the crown can suddenly take arms against their sovereign.'

'Calm down, father!' Catharine spoke quietly but with some bite. 'Anyway, what are you up to, George Bowman? I presume that Bowman is your name. If you are working for the king as well then we need to work out the safest way for this to work'. She giggled suddenly. 'I keep saying the word 'work' don't I?'

George and Ned exchanged glances. They both took a sip of beer. 'Let's work it out!' George decided.

CHAPTER 14

War Stories

❖ ❖ ❖

THE BOYS WERE BACK AT the charcoal burner's. 'So, Ezekial', George said, sitting on a log and peering up at the little man who seemed never to sit down. 'You fought with my father.'

'Yes, George and Sir William. It were a long time ago. Let me tell you about it...' Ned sat up eager as a school boy. Indeed, the only part of school that he had liked had been the stories - preferably fairy tales or Greek myths, not so much the bible stories. Easy strode about the little clearing waving his hands 'Howard de Vere was our commander and we were just boys like you, fighting for our king - sort of- with a raggle-taggle bunch of Germans and what-have-you. We were in the siege of Mannheim in the year 20. The huge Spanish army was camped outside and our numbers were thin. Very thin.' His hands described the German town and its modest defenders. George could see the sparkle of Ned's eyes drinking in every word. ' We tried everything to convince the Spaniard that there was a full garrison. Dead men propped on the walls. Boys like me firing off five muskets at once. The one thing we had enough of was powder. Your father and I spent every evening making up bombs. And it were a bomb of ours that blew off Sir William's leg too'. He looked a bit sad for a minute. Ned made haste to give him a mug of small beer. They had brought as much small beer and provisions as they could carry. That had been part of the plan they had hatched.

'To cut a long story short, after three weeks we were coming to the end of our tether. We decided to break out while we still had the strength. We had eaten all the dogs, and the cats and the horse. We had nearly finished the rats.

'Obviously, we had plenty of water and as much powder as we might wish for. There were thirty or forty youngsters willing to go and Hopton, the present commander, to lead us. He was no older than us really but quality. He'd had experience too, a soldier from 15 - even younger than you two.

'We chose a moonlit night so that we could dispense with lights. We had bundles of bombs and, in passing, we were going to blow up whatever we could - their powder store, some guns, a wagon or two. We crept out of the city, down trenches and ramparts. For a while, it was as though the enemy had gone to sleep. There was no one. The world had ended, it felt like, and in the pale moonlight, all that was left was mud and the stink of too many people.'

He paused, gazing upwards like he could see it all in his mind's eye. He stirred the food cooking in his cauldron. 'Then all hell broke loose' and Easy stamped his foot and the boys jumped, like he had intended.

At that moment, several horsemen burst into the clearing. There was a moment of silence - the two boys and Ezekial round their cooking fire and the snorting horses with armoured men upon their backs. 'We saw some soldiers come in here', one of the troopers finally said.

'We ain't seen no one', George answered, exaggerating his accent and pitching his voice loud enough to be heard over the swishing foliage and heavily breathing horses. The horses swivelled round with a clink of bridle and a stamp of foot. Without another word, they rushed away again. George thought that maybe it was like a game for the cavalry as well. Rush rush, get nothing done. There was another, quieter, rustling and the slightly sheepish face of Sam the sarjent appeared.

'I thought I was going to be forced to listen to all of Ezekial's tall tales. You were far too young to have been at the siege of Mannheim you old fraud. If you served with Hopton, it must have been later'.

Ezekial laughed, a foxy bark. 'Maybe I'm not remembering it right', he declared. 'Have some stew sarjent! We have news of a sort and await your instructions'. He made a mock bow as though the fancy language was from some stage play. For some reason, George and Ned stood and bowed as well.

'Fancy, you lot have become', the sarjent laughed. 'Let's get down to business' and they all sat down again, even Easy. 'Our army is going to have to come up this very hill. It is almost impossible to rush an entrenched force up a hill but we might be able to manage it. We need to sneak the whole army up through the woodlands and the stands of trees. When we reach the top, we will still have a huge job.

'We need you two to work out a route for most of the army. We need it marked and when the battle starts we will need you to lead the war parties or they're sure as houses to get themselves bleeding lorst.

'Any questions?' There was a bit of a silence. A few twigs fell. The clouds marched across the sky. There was a very distant sound of a horse's hooves.

'My uncle is in charge of the party camped up here', George admitted miserably. He picked up his long bow and dug it in the soft ground.

'A few years ago, the King suggested that everyone learn to use a long bow. Was that how you came to be the only bowman in the army?'

'Absolutely not. I had my first bow when I was eight'. George looked cross but Sam had deflected him from his misery.

'Don't worry about your uncle. All of us have friends or relatives on the other side. That is why they say that the world is upside down. Nobody knows where they stand.'

There was another loud drum-roll of horses' hooves, coming nearer and nearer. The sarjent faded away like smoke. One moment he was talking and the next, the earlier scene was repeated. This time it was four horsemen in the clearing. The leader looked to be the same one. He had, George noticed, a very white scar under one eye, like a splash of lime mortar.

'We couldn't find anyone anywhere', he declared angrily to the now familiar jingle of bridle and clinking of weapons.

'Which side you be on?' George asked.

'We are troopers upholding Parliament and the King', the man answered.

'You be against the King then?' George worried that he was overdoing the yokel act. The man sounded like a Londoner but you never can tell. Maybe he was from Kent. Didn't hurt to ask. 'You from Kent then?'

The horsemen left again without answering George's questions. 'Rude bastards', George said in his broadest accent. Easy and Ned laughed themselves silly. George didn't think it was so very funny but there was an undeniable tension whenever the enemy cavalry appeared.

'How are we going to mark the route?' George asked, really to stop their stupid laughter. They talked for a while.

The light had leeched from the sky when there was a rustle of leaves and Catharine's head popped up. 'Hello', she whispered. George got up and went over to her.

'What are you doing here?' he asked and realised that it might sound a little rude. 'Is it safe?'

'I had to dodge your uncle's patrol, twice. But I doubt they care about any farm girl.'

'What about your father? Won't he be concerned?'

'It's his message. He wants to see you tomorrow morning - come and get a load of wood. We have a special collection of ash for the final run of the charcoal. Do say you'll come!' She suddenly seemed, for the first time, girlish, enthusiastic, silly. George found it charming.

'Ned could come', he told her, pretending a lack of interest and risking (it felt like) everything. Her face clouded over but then, in the half-light, there was a radiant smile and she gave him a quick kiss on the lips.

No Sleep on Landsdowne

❖ ❖ ❖

HE STOOD THERE, AGES AFTER she had left, the kiss burning on his lips. It was fully dark when finally Ned shouted, quietly, 'come on you nitwit! She went hours ago'. Dreamily and strangely, George floated back to their camp beds, nestling close up against the charcoal clamp, which gave a slow gentle heat and an occasional belch all through the night.

George knew about the clamp's noises - and all about the other night sounds - because he slept not one wink. There were owls and farting (mostly from Ezekial) and little creatures scurrying; hedgehogs snuffled and the wind got up just before dawn and dew fell, not quite soundlessly but so quietly it was like the kiss of an angel or a kiss from Catharine. And, of course, it was this simple kiss that kept him thinking so stupidly. How many children might they have? What should be their names? Do you re-use the names of children that had died? George was the third 'George' born to his parents - the other two did not make it to their first birthday and were buried in High Ham graveyard.

Finally, it was time to get up. Ned stared into his face, frowned and said, 'you've got it bad'. George did not reply. He did not know whether Ned should come with him or Ezekial. The patrols knew they were all charcoal burners. There was nothing odd or surprising for all of them to go to the farm, except that someone should be keeping an eye. The clamp was at its most critical phase. Today, it needed to be stuffed up with the alder that would make the best charcoal. Ezekial had half an alder tree trunk in its heart but around this core was needed smaller hard wood and, in his view, oak was best. George was amused at himself for caring about the charcoal. It was as if he could not help it.

As it happened, Ezekial and the wagon, with George holding the reins, lumbered into the farm yard. The two old men hugged and slapped each other's back and laughed deep booming laughs. George and Catharine started shy but loading the wagon thawed them out. Soon, she was chucking huge lumps of oak up at him and he was urging her to throw them higher and faster.

They'd loaded up and no sign of the 'old men'. George gave her an impromptu demonstration with his bow. He chose (and why not?) the impossible shot of a pigeon on the wing. More by luck than judgement, he got one through the wings and it fell a few hundred yards away. They rushed off laughing and when he picked up the bird, she kissed him again. They held each other for a moment. George could feel his heart hammering like a blacksmith's anvil, bang bang bang. After a while, he realised it was also gun shots. They hurried back to the farm house.

Easy and Sir William were firing old guns into the air. 'There are soldiers around', George shouted. The two 'old men' looked as guilty as schoolboys.

'Sorry, George. You're right. We got to talking about the old days and needs must we find our old weapons. His voice was rather more 'educated' talking to Sir William. He turned to that old gentleman. 'It might be worth you showing George your 'Science room', sir'.

'If you think so Ezekial'. Sir William did not seem very keen but led George through the house to a chamber at the back with large windows of expensive glass and not much of a view into the kitchen garden and the side of the hill. George rubbed his eyes. His sleepless night was telling on him. Then he rubbed them again in amazement. On the long trestle tables were the oddest collection of objects that he had ever seen.

'Science, science', he muttered to himself, never having heard the word. But as his eyes took in the strange array of crucibles and retort stands, the pungent sulphurous smoke, the instruments that he had never seen before for purposes about which he could hardly even guess, suddenly he understood. 'Natural philosophy', he said out loud.

'Indeed, indeed', chuckled Sir William warming to the task. 'Some of it has practical applications and some of it does not. You will like this one here'.

With extreme care, he handed George a metal tube that clinked and settled as he took it. He gently moved it around in his hands. Was it a gun? A method for starting fires? The metal felt cold but there was something heavier inside it that rattled faintly. Exquisite care had been put into the making of it and George handled it like a day-old chick.

'That cost two fields', Catharine had come in with some hot milk and honey. Her look to her father was tender but exasperated. 'He felt he had to have a second one'.

'If you were very careful, you might perhaps borrow it', Sir William's voice had a strange mixture of pride and reluctance. 'If you were very careful', he repeated, perhaps already regretting the offer.

'But what is it?' George sounded a little bit cross. It was as though they were teasing him.

'Look through the small hole', Sir William took the tube and pit it to his eye. He pointed it out of the window. Then he helped George hold it the right way round looking through the rippled glass. He gasped and took it from his eye and put it back and gasped again. Catharine laughed, a deep rich gurgle, and he turned to look at her flashing eye and the mouth he wished again to kiss. Sir William coughed and began to explain the 'telescope', as he claimed it had recently been named, in Italy.

George wanted to tell Ned again and again that he, George, had been lent the telescope. Ned had promised that he was looking for 'only a moment'. In fact, it was difficult for George to get back the gadget at all. The two of them stood on exactly the top of the hill where they expected the battle. In front of them was a low wall, stark in the strong sunlight, but if they were careful, they could see through a gap and remain hidden in the woods. They were in the shadows of an old elm, buckled by time and, perhaps, the movement of the earth down the steep hill.

'There's that cavalry patrol', Ned whispered, although there was no one within miles. 'Have a quick look!' George glimpsed the horses - perhaps three miles away on the plain - before the instrument was snatched from his eye. 'And I think that the main body of their army is drawing up. We will have to go to the wall.' They slowly crept up to the wall and Ned looked through the glass. George realised that Ned was making a mistake but was too slow to stop him. The sun had glinted off the lens and the cavalry was galloping towards them.

What could they do? George dragged Ned down. 'What can we do?' he said, his voice strangely loud.

'Kill them!' was Ned's inevitable answer.

'What? Twenty people on horses? Do you have a cannon on you?'

'Use your medallion'.

'What are you talking about?' George stared around. There was a faint sound of galloping horses. They had one minute left before they were discovered. The stone wall in front of George was suddenly in super-sharp focus, as though he were using the telescope on it. Time slowed to a crawl. A beetle made its way between the lichened limestone, its antenna trembling like a feather. George felt Ned grabbing at his clothes. For a second, he thought his friend had gone crazy.

'Your amulet. Quickly, give it to me'.

The boys hid in the wood, exactly where they had prepared the positions for the advance guard of the army. Even while they waited nervously, the noises somehow magnified despite the wall, George admired the logs and undergrowth they had arranged to hide dozens of troops. After a while, the cavalry troop thundered away presumably to meddle annoyingly somewhere else. George and Ned emerged and quietly approached the wall. The amulet on its leather thong was gone. They slowly climbed the wall. There were tiny rustlings of stone and lichen. Ned gave George a warning look. Ned, as usual, was quicker, nimbler. He was poised on the top edge, wicked dagger drawn when a sword skewered up between his legs. How exactly Ned avoided having his genitals run through, George did not know. The effort of turning, leaping, twisting certainly had him fall like a sack of new-fangled potatoes down the other side. There was a bang, then silence.

On the Wall

❖　❖　❖

GEORGE LOOKED OVER THE WALL to try to see Ned and was suddenly staring into the nastiest face he had ever seen. The face expressed surprise – slitty eyes opened to their full extent, an old scar from right eye to chin gleaming whitely, blondy-ginger beard pushing through a grey city-folk pallor – and then the thin mouth opened and a swear word emerged through dark brown teeth. George hit it with his quiver. It was not a serious blow, it was not even a very good blow but the man ('Scarface' George named him instantly) fell over and George had notched up and was aiming down before he'd recovered.

The man lay staring at George. The look was sneering but also coldly assessing. 'Your medallion', the man said with a Midlands accent, throwing the amulet. It wrapped around the arrow and, when the arrow was loosed, pulled it wide, even at the very short range. The man kicked at George and ran, Ned's dagger missing him by a whisker. Round the side of the wall there was a whinny, shouted commands and one horse's hooves drumming. Scarface rode like the wind, keeping the contours between him and the boys. George and Ned ran onto the plain, a breeze at their backs.

'I thought you'd been shot', George cried to his friend but Ned just shook his head.

They had been on the plain for nearly a week. George had spent every second, unconsciously, scanning the landscape. He found he knew every fold and kink, every dip and rise. He turned almost 90 degrees from the sounds of the horse, waited for ten seconds, and began firing so fast that he was a blur. He had six arrows in the air in just over a minute and eagle-eyed Ned could just see them dropping a hundred yards away. Ned's thoughts, always murderous, became murderous with disappointment just as Scarface's horse raced into the descending arrows and flickered, spinning out of sight. Ned ran.

Ned could move as silently as a deer. He found the horse, dying, riderless, bristling with arrows. Its gasps rasped, until they stopped. Now, he followed the blood trail without even the swish of grasses. It was not because he was worried about alerting his prey - to some extent he did not care if the deer, the rabbit, the pike, the human knew he was coming. He padded silent as sleeping breath because his ears were pricked up, scanning, scanning, like his eyes. Perhaps more than his eyes - eyes were concentrating on the ground, tracking the spoor of blood, looking forward, making lines. Ears were doing something different. They were picking up and sorting a panoply of subtle sounds. With the wind behind him, his ears were going to struggle.

They still caught the tiny scream - from the farm.

It is hard to judge the speed of a hunter's brain. He spent a long time - perhaps a second - evaluating the importance of the noise and correlating it to the blood spots. After the second and without any more hesitation, he ran like a long distance runner, straight to the farm. He arrived at the same time as George, who had gone half as far and who was red-faced and panting. Ned ignored his friend and raced straight into the parlour. He noted (eyes quickly adjusting to the gloom) the chair knocked over, the tiny, well-nigh invisible drops of blood and a whimpering.

He arrived in the 'science room' to find death scattered everywhere. Behind him, heavier, louder, George stumbled in and then cried out. 'Catharine, Catharine! Help me Ned!' But Ned was concerned with other things - the chase. Was Scarface still in the room? Was he still in the house? The dead kittens scattered on the floor did not concern him. He spared them a brief glance and no more. Catharine's dead father scarcely got a flicker extra. Ned's eyes lingered very briefly on the man's open eyes, staring, sightless. Finally, his gaze swept over to Catharine, covered in blood and lying as lifeless as a rag doll. With an inward sigh, he went over reluctantly to help. So much less fun than chasing his prey!

In the darkest corner of that bright room, Catharine's white dress and white skin shone. The blood looked almost black. George was crying over her, tears, Ned noticed, actually falling on the linen of her dress. He gently pushed George aside and put his hand under her nose, as though to let her smell him. 'She's still alive', Ned told George in his normal quiet voice.

When George did not respond, he smacked his friend and said in a much louder voice, shouting for Ned really, 'she's alive you bumbling oaf. Pick her up!'

George's face cleared slightly. Still a bit like an automaton, he lifted her up, so very carefully, cushioning her head. Ned cleared one of the work benches and George placed her, like a china doll, on the top. And, like a china doll, her eyes suddenly opened. 'Dad, dad', she cried, trying to rise. George held her gently down.

'He's dead, I'm afraid.' There was no easier way to say it. Her face screwed up and she howled. George kept his hands on her shoulders and Ned left.

There was an odd pause, as though the world was holding its breath. George, holding tight to Catharine, found stray thoughts running through his head. He very much liked hugging the girl and felt guilty because he thought he shouldn't. He looked at the spread of dead kittens and wondered what sort of man would kill them. And then, he saw that the best telescope was missing. 'Ned', he cried, quite softly because of the girl upon his chest. Ned appeared straight away. 'Scarface has stolen the telescope', George told him and Catharine lifted her head and looked at him.

'Really?' she asked. 'That makes sense - otherwise why kill father. What about the kittens?'

There was a pause and then Ned it was who replied, 'I think er, I think that they simply got in his way. Like your dad. I think he came here to steal the instrument. I think he worked out that we had one. Maybe he had snuck around the house

earlier.' It was the longest speech George had ever heard from
his friend. He felt huge gratitude and tears formed in his eyes.
He dashed them away with his hand - no time for that now.

It was agony for Ned, the waiting. He paced up and down for
a while. He went outside, stared at the coins of sunlight falling between the trees, the breath of wind stirring the leaves.
Everything he looked at increased his impatience. The good
weather reminded him of how the army needed to hurry. The
breeze was from the right direction. After a while, he realised
that some of his discomfort was because he was worrying about
his friend. This made him stop his pacing for a moment. He felt
that he'd never had to worry about someone else before. He
had, he knew, worried when he'd started school but that was
worry about and for himself. Soon enough, George had made
it all better. Now, he could not make it better for George. He
wondered whether he had rushed over to the army command
in order to avoid the dead farmer, the mourning farm, his dev-
astated friend.

When the aide finally called him through, Ned's face had a
thoughtful frown, unusual for him. Sir David was there and Sir
Hopton. They were eating pomegranates and offered some to
Ned on a small plate with a knife on it. Ned did not know what
the fruit was and refused, but accepted a glass of wine absently.
Sir David asked him to explain what the boys had seen and

what they'd done. Sir Hopton listened with barely concealed disdain, eating tiny pieces of dark red flesh.

'I don't really care what your boys have been doing', he declared rudely, spraying red juice, before adding, too late, 'no offence intended'. And, in fact, Ned was thinking too hard to take offence. He was, for that second, not thinking about the coming battle. He was thinking about his feelings for his friend. He sipped his wine with a distant look in his eye.

'Where's George?' Sir David finally asked.

Ned didn't answer. He was checking through what they had done to prepare. He wished George was there to chat about it. They had cleared a path for the troops up the left hand side of the very steep hill. No one need get killed on the middle of the hill. At the top of the piece of woodland, they had created a barricade behind which the attackers could wait in relative safety. But no plan survived the first shot, as George's dad would often say.

CHAPTER 16

Let Battle Commence

❖ ❖ ❖

NED WAS NEAR THE TOP of an ash tree with bullets pattering around him. He looked down with no concern for his own skin. 'Four hundred and twenty three', he shouted down. George huddled behind the trunk at the bottom shook his head in disbelief. There were so many things he could not believe.

Most of all, here they were as had been predicted. George and Ned were trying to get the Royalist foot-soldiers (who fancied themselves the best thing since baked bread) up the steep hill towards the wall at the top. Obviously, the parliamentarians were trying to stop the King's army and it was easy for them to do so.

In front of him, George could see the legs and torsos of soldiers struggling up the steep hill. He was in a part of Weston wood directly below the dry stone wall at which his amulet had saved them. He watched Royalists clamber and he watched Royalists die.

'Four hundred and forty', Ned shouted.

There were now 440 soldiers not moving on the steep slope and it was all Sir Hopton's fault. The Royalist's commander had not listened to Ned and he had not listened to Sir David. George was filled with a murderous rage as, not ten yards away, a man's head appeared to explode. He was plucked backwards out of sight, cart-wheeling over a pile of his comrades and leaving another splatter of blood on an already blood-stained scene.

George said, his anger like a lump in his throat, 'I am going to do something right now'.

'Sir Hopton gave us specific instructions', Ned muttered from his position in the trees.

'That's as maybe', George shouted, suddenly on fire with rage, 'he's murdering our troops'.

'Four hundred and forty five'. The rate that men were dying had slowed down. Mostly because almost no one was moving up the slope. The sarjent joined them.

'They'll run away if we do nothing', Sam declared. 'They've taken awful punishment. It's a miracle they ain't run already. I'll get the officer in charge', he muttered and went off running crab-like into the swathe of bullets.

Actually, George noticed, there were hardly any bullets coming down through the thirty yard gap. The roundheads were happy to stay leaning over the wall picking them off slowly now the rush was over. Ned lightly leapt from ten foot up, landing on his feet. George could see the anger in his eyes. 'I'm going to do something', George told him. There was almost silence. Even the screaming had briefly quieted.

'What do you mean by this?' the officer demanded, spittle flecking his moustache and pointed beard. 'We have orders and you are disobeying them'. As silently as a snake, Ned had his dagger in the man's throat. George went up to him and whispered in his ear.

'You are going to do what we say or you are going to die right here, right now. If you understand, nod your head'. There was a barely perceptible nod, the man's eyes showing the whites.

'Order the troops to come in here, as loud as you can'.

The officer found his voice, strangled at first, then louder, he shouted, 'Everyone over here at the double'. Sam, miles louder, shouted the order again and again. Men started pouring into the woodland. George and Ned began the job of getting them safely up the hill. Sam took the officer off their hands.

George, Ned and the sarjent were at the top of the wood, looking across at the dry stone wall with its mostly hidden defenders. 'Your preparations have worked well', Sam said approvingly, 'Now, we have to dislodge them'.

Behind them were about two hundred soldiers, all that could fit in really, with another two hundred waiting behind. Only thirty or so could get their muskets aligned in the right direction but another thirty were ready for the second volley. At present, all the soldiers were hidden behind the logs that George and Ned had prepared. George looked round at them. Most were grinning. Most had blood on their faces. They were as excited as school boys because they could see that they were going to get their own back at the roundheads. No sign of fear at all.

The sunlight flickered through the leaves and George almost fell asleep. The key moment was very soon but tiredness suddenly overwhelmed him. He had a strange flickering dream about Catharine and the telescope and Scarface. Then he was being roughly shaken and the nasty taste of Ned's glove was on his mouth. He looked at his friend in a sudden panic but remembered where they were. He hoped to hell that Sam would get the timing right.

Ned crept from the wood and snuck under the shelter of the wall, so the enemy could not see him. They had gathered undergrowth in a tunnel previously but only Ned was small enough to do it. Ned crouched under the top of the wall and slowly inched his arms up. Then, with a jerk, he began pulling muskets out of the enemy's hands and chucking them down the slope. One discharged with a crack and the ball whined overhead. The shouts were comical. 'Oi', 'watch out', 'get off you bastard'. George could see Ned smiling. George had a strange memory of a football match he had witnessed once down Langport high street. 'Over here'. 'Watch it'. 'Get him'

Ned was able to tear away seven or eight muskets before the enemy soldiers began jumping on the wall to stop him. George stepped out of the woodland and shot them. Bows and arrows are not soundless. There was the twang and the thwack and the gurgling and the thump. But, for those behind the wall, it was a mystery. Most of those hit by arrows fell down the slope, tumbling like acrobats with no bones, past the stacks of Royal dead. Even those who fell on the enemy side of the wall meant nothing. Who was expecting a bowman? Most of them had hardly seen an arrow before, unless they were country people. Ned stood up and began knocking over the soldiers standing on the wall by swinging his pike end carefully.

Finally, some more intelligent parliamentarian understood. 'It's an archer', the man shouted, his voice broken and hoarse from the musket smoke, 'rush him'. Thirty enemy troops got up on the wall and George hid behind it. Thirty muskets boomed and, from this range, most hit their mark. A score of round-heads fell, sounding like sacks of grain dropped onto a wagon.

The enemy voice shouted, 'next rank, to the wall' but they did not know where the fire was coming from and they stuck head and gun too high. The next volley killed half of them. George gestured at Sam. Through the gunpowder smoke, their eyes met. Sam nodded (weirdly in slow-motion, George thought). He could see the sarjent yelling and the Royalists began scrambling to the wall and over it but all sound had gone. An enemy musket must have discharged right by his ear but he never saw it. He got up, leaving bow and arrows behind, slowly climbed the wall like an old man. Royalists were jumping, leaping and dying all around him. But so were the enemy. He moved in a sudden patch of complete silence watching mouths screaming silently, swords clashing noiselessly and the mayhem of hand-to-hand conducted like an elaborate dance but without music. He stood there and gawped at Ned, whirling like the dervish he was. His pike ripped great holes in the enemy ranks as he spun it. Sam was running and shouting, a mad grin on his face, chopping time and again with his sword.

The enemy could not take it. They were no more real soldiers than the Royalists but their morning had been spent shooting down at people slowly ascending the steep hill. No more tiring than killing sitting ducks. And these ducks couldn't even fly! Now, things had changed. The enemy, black with powder and savage with glee, had appeared from nowhere and these Royalists were flying at them! All the 'prentices, all the clerks, all the townsfolk that had joined the rebellion, they had a vision of dying at the wall. The wall had changed from their bosom friend to their arch enemy. They ran. The hoarse-voiced officer shouted at them to stop. He was shot by twenty muskets. The second and third wave had climbed the wall and suddenly George's hearing came back and he could hear bugles and shouting to show that the whole army - four thousand men - were coming up the hill. Sam was shouting for the wall to be dismantled and a fire-step built on the far side, effectively turning its potential around so that the Royalists could fire across the plain. Three hundred men did the job in ten minutes.

George passed out again.

CHAPTER 17

Quick, Quick, Do Nothing

❖ ❖ ❖

GEORGE CAME TO, WITH SOMETHING irritating his head. There was a tugging and a painful scrape. He had visions of ravens ravenously feasting on his scalp. 'I'm not dead', he shouted and tried to rise, his hands windmilling round his head.

'There, there', a voice said, as though he were a tricky horse. 'Of course, you're not dead'. But his eyes were pointed down the hill, through a gap in the dismantled wall, and flocks of ravens were indeed feasting on the dead. His eyes focused better. Most of the 'ravens' were black-garbed women and they were helping the fallen. He turned his head carefully. 'A bullet just scraped along your skull' Catharine told him. It was Catharine! How could she be here?

'How could you be here?' he tried to ask but all that came out was a hoarse croak. She gave him some water. 'How could you be here?' he repeated. He stared at her blinding white clothing. She was like something from his dreams.

She gave him the assessing look that nurses had always managed. She judged him 'back to normal' and helped him to sit up. 'I came over to see what I could do', she told him 'and lucky I did too. You were face down when I found 'ee. You could have choked'.

There was a commotion nearby and rough words, which Catharine made no sign of hearing, and then Catharine was forcibly pulled back and a worried voice shouted, 'is he here?' A small face pressed itself near George and he wasn't sure if he hadn't heard a sob. It was Ned.

'Are you crying Ned?' George asked. Catharine was smiling and bustling round.

'I've got some food, I'll just bring it for you'. She went the other side of the wall.

'What's happening?' George asked. He stood up, swayed a little and then sat on the half wall. In front of him were mostly parliamentarian dead. The black-garbed women seemed to be stealing anything they could find. George wondered briefly how people remembered these sorts of skills in the decades of peace. Robbing corpses. Thieving from dead soldiers. Perhaps it was something that came as natural to humans as breathing.

Catharine returned and offered bread and cheese to the boys, undoing the linen kerchief wrapping. She had a jug of cider and this went down first and fast. Ned began talking quietly, 'they went over there; we chased them'. And that was all he said.

There was a silence. George and Catharine were wondering if Ned was really going to leave it at that. There was a wailing of women and the injured. A light smattering of bridle rattling and the clinking of weapons. And, miracle of miracles, Ned spoke some more. 'They're coming back'. Beyond the first miracle, was the second. Ned shouted, eyes gleaming with a happiness that George had never seen in another human being, 'THEY ARE COMING BACK'. Catharine and the other women faded back into the woodland.

Instantly, the officers and sergeants began rousing their men. A ragged line of musketeers appeared on the Landsdowne side of the wall and pike men in front of it, including George and Ned. George noticed that Sam had appeared as well and the old sarjent winked and muscled in next to them. 'Glad to see you up and about, Georgie boy! I'll take it from here'. And he stepped out of the line and began a shouting which silenced the whole line. 'Pike men stand up, butt end down. BUTT END DOWN, you bladdy plough boys'. He soon had a fairly straight, dressed line. There was a drumming from behind him but he did not turn round. 'When I give the command, you pike men will LIE DOWN and the musketeers will fire a volley. If you are too slow, they will shoot you. DO NOT MOVE 'TIL I COMMAND!'

The drumming got louder and louder. George glanced down the line and could see eyes wide as plates in dirty faces. He laughed and caught Ned's eye. How could Ned look <u>even</u> happier! He was radiating joy and his laugh, while much quieter, was a frightening thing. The cavalry charge was nearly upon them. Without the sarjent, George knew that they would have all hid behind the wall and maybe that would not have mattered. The enemy horses, muzzles flecked with foam and the enemy horsemen, shouting wildly through a variety of facial hair, were twenty yards away when Sam gave the order and dived down himself. There was a crash of musketry and the enemy horses stopped like they had hit a wall. One pike man had been too slow and was shot by his own side. He was thrown forwards under the collapsing legs of a dying horse.

'Get UP PIKES', Sam bellowed, his own beard flecked with spit. He pushed into the line and up came the pikes. The scattering of horses on their feet would not come near the bristling metal. The unhorsed riders tried to attack with swords but they were useless against pikes. An enemy infantry detachment was on its way, running towards them dragging their own pikes but they were not an immediate threat. 'Walk forward, pike men' Sam commanded and this time, for whatever reason, it was like a parade ground. A hundred men paced forward, in perfect time, found their way past the dead horses, killing a few roundheads in passing, and formed up the other side of the failed charge. George noticed that the ground fell away very gently.

Sam had these men completely ready. Silent. Totally focused. There was a longer pause. A veteran muttered, 'hurry up, do nothing' in a voice that was giggly with pleasure. George felt it and sighed with wonder. It was not just Ned. Every man jack of them was loving it. A chance to stuff the enemy. They'd done it once and it was pleasure beyond price. George could see that it made being with a woman, for these men, a very poor second best. When the enemy pike men had come near enough, Sam did it again.

Maybe it was his head wound but George saw and heard the next engagement in slow motion. Sam's mouth opened and words and spit flew from his mouth (George had time to guess it was 'Lie down pikes'). George himself was first down and he bounced and then watched the line of men all bouncing the same, small amount. The bark of the muskets was as slow as the popping corn from America he had once been shown by a drunken sailor. The blood darted from the enemy wounds like silk streamers and their cries could have been from gulls or the ravens that circled above. There was even a bit of the song 'greensleaves' in his ears

He stood again and time speeded up. The Royalists were getting tired. Most of them had climbed the hill under heavy fire only a few hours before. Most of them had minor wounds, like George's. There was blood on many a face. This time, as they advanced, there were stumbles aplenty, foul swearing and the peculiar sound of pike thumping through a body. The pike men, when the pike had gone through an enemy, had to continue advancing but with a sword or cutlass or knife in hand. The line broke down into individual fights. In fact, the Royalist amateurs were faring very poorly against the well-trained band of roundheads, despite the massive number advantage when...

Sam shouted again. 'Kingsmen disengage. One step back. And drop'. George guessed as he again threw himself down that this was the hardest possible manoeuvre. Indeed, most Royal pikes managed but plenty did not. The musket volley was, of course, indiscriminate but when the pikemen got up again, the enemy fled...

Into a charge of horse. George was sick. His foes had been in front of him one moment, the next they had been swept away as from the broom of a house-proud shop-keeper. The Royal horse swept through them and left but scraps on the ground and an agonising smack, echoing in the air below the thunder of hooves. The Royal pikemen collapsed in exhaustion, as though ordered by Sam, and left Sam alone looking out across the plain.

'That went well', Sam muttered, perhaps to himself and a lonely flute began to play the tune, 'follow the drum' until told to shut up, in much stronger language. The wind got up a little and sweat dried. Clouds inched across a sky turning darker blue, almost indigo. George passed out again.

CHAPTER 18

Ruder

❖ ❖ ❖

THE NEXT AWAKENING WAS MUCH ruder. No starched linen skirts.
No clean smells of dairy and country air. No soft voice. George
was slapped awake with heavy blows of a gauntleted hand.
'Wake up you bastard. Get on your feet! Face the commander
now.'

It was the officer from the hill and he was mad as hell.
George could feel his spittle falling on his face like a thin

drizzle. He was hauled to his feet and stood there swaying. He could taste the mud and leather of the man's glove. He felt sick.

'Did you stop this officer in the performance his duties?' the supercilious voice of Sir Hopton asked.

George squinted up at a man on a horse. 'Answer the commander you scum!' the officer shouted.

'Gerald, please, let the yokel speak!' There was silence.

'Yes but..' George began but he was immediately knocked off his feet again as 'Gerald' shouted that he was under arrest. There was plenty more shouting and George found himself flung under a wagon right by the famous wall. The wall had featured a huge amount in his life recently, George thought, and he went to sleep.

Soon afterwards, there was a whispering that penetrated his dreams and Catharine was saying his name. 'Yes' he answered, mouth as thick as an old stocking. And then it was Ned talking. He talked for a very long time – for him - and several times George had to ask him to repeat stuff. Sir David was unconscious and therefore no help. Prince Rupert had buggered off towards Bristol. It was in the middle of the biggest battle on English soil for a hundred and fifty years and they were wasting time arresting him, little old George Bowman, sweet sixteen and properly kissed twice. George shook his head – his thoughts were all over the place. 'Come back in an hour' he told Ned. He needed time to think.

Looking out from under the wagon was much like being in a box at the theatre, although George had never experienced the theatre himself. His teacher, the Reverend Dodd, had been an avid fan of plays, despite his calling as a man of God. Perhaps it was this most of all had made George keen to fight for the King. He'd loved those stories of the London theatres, of Shakespeare's theatres forty years before. Some of the Roundheads wanted to close the theatres.

But it was very beautiful and not unlike the show that George had seen outside 'The Bear' at Curry Rival fair. In between Punch and Judy (so very violent, so very rude), there had been a man presenting 'The Battle of Bosworth Field' and 'The Spanish Armada'. In them days, George's dad could afford the outrageous price of a penny for each performance. And, in them days, they had happily watched paper armies cross wooden fields to the sound effects of cocoa-nuts and penny whistles. Now George had his own show - 'The Battle of Landsdowne' 4th of July 1643. Or was it the 5th? The cart he was under made a perfect frame as cavalry, as small as paper cut-outs, swept from one side of the plain to the other, under a painted sky. The puffs of smoke, no bigger than a match-strike, echoed slow as a finger tapping on a wooden box. The mass of foot-soldiers advanced, retreated, advanced again. All that was missing was the show-man's careful explanation, rather like the vicar's voice, George now thought, his mind wondering.

George felt almost guilty. Catharine could not be far away. He was so comfortable and happy under his wagon - all he needed was a cup of the hideously expensive 'cha' (or tea as some people were beginning to call it) and the telescope. Where was the telescope? He supposed that light-fingered Ned had 'borrowed' it again. He did not care. His eyes closed slowly, the sun shone and moved across the sky, until his face was lit; he slept. Catharine found him - could not be bothered to wake him.

She needed Ned anyway.

Catharine had found out a number of things. George's new enemy (and therefore hers as well) was Sir Hopton (really Sir Ralph Hopton's) nephew, Gerald, the officer Ned had threatened. Sir Ralph, with no children of his own, had named the lad his heir and given him a company to command. His name was Gerald Granger and he was not well liked. Except by his uncle. Catharine wrinkled her brows. That was the problem. She still had not found Sir David, nor Prince Rupert. She could hardly take Sam from the pike wall which was now guarding the whole baggage train of the army.

Ned had to stop being a soldier for a minute and find George some help. Catharine was entirely happy to knock out or kill the guards - she had plenty of farm servants who could do the job for her. Acker Pensford would be willing. Bill Bythesea would love it. Even Peter at a pinch. However, no employee would make it possible for George to carry on his job. As a spy. Catharine knew - perhaps only she knew - that George and Ned had won this battle for the King. The pretty marching and bright array of horse-men was just so much glitter and sparkle. The storming of the wall had left the Roundheads nowhere to go. They had lost. They simply had not realised it yet. The marching and charging were as much use in the real world as a children's show.

However, Ned had to find Sir David and, if possible, Prince Rupert. It was no use her, a girl, traipsing through the army.

She would get rude comments or ruder actions. Ned was quick and sharp and, if George was to be believed, could look after himself. Indeed, she thought George's attitude to his friend had a healthy measure of fear.

It was strange and interesting being on the edge of a battle. There were encounters occurring both to the left, more towards Bristol way, and to the right, in the direction of Devizes, say. At this distance, the sights were breath-takingly beautiful she thought. She gave a little sob and then pulled herself together. This was no moment for remembering her dad – his peculiar mixture of interests. His extreme love of beauty, wherever it might be found. His fiddling with new inventions.

To some extent, she knew, she was deliberately wasting time. She was waiting for Ned to re-appear. There was no point dashing off to find him. He knew that he had to come back here. And, finally, as if on cue but very tardy, there he was.

'Ned, Ned' she went over eagerly, grasped his arm. His clothes were an extraordinary mess. He seemed to be covered in a mixture of mud, straw, blood and worse. She wanted to pick the rubbish off him.

His response was to look at her coldly, as though they had never met. A few milli-seconds of this and she dropped her arm but his face changed and there was an actual smile. 'Catharine', he whispered, 'good to see you'.

'We need to help George now', she declared.

It would be fair to say, Ned thought, that, on the whole, he did not like using his brain. He loved hunting – was an absolute star in his own opinion – because he single-mindedly chased the prey. Easy. 'Looking', on the other hand, not so good. He was, as his mother was fond of telling him, a 'boy looker'. Asked to find the pepper, a very expensive and useful thing, carefully put away from a casual thief, Ned found nothing at all. He would return, like boys from time immemorial, with the words that could be on every male tombstone – the whining 'I can't find it'.

He knew it was pathetic.

However, he debated with himself, as he searched through tent after tent in pursuit of Sir David, dead or alive, only he himself could find Sir David. There was no choice. He had run through Catharine's logic three or four times, while his short and rapid legs took him down hill and up dale, through wagon train, field kitchen, munition dump, arsenal, smithy corner, brothel, stabling to finally find the barber-surgeons. There was no flaw. It was him or no one.

Thank God, he felt, finally, when he succeeded. There was a light in Catharine's eye he found very scary. It was emotional and close to tears. He did not like it.

'Sir David', he whispered, dropping to his knees next to a pallette-bed. 'Sir David', he repeated. The spymaster opened his eyes and the orderly behind Ned warned Ned not to be too long.

'Sir David', Ned said for the third time.

CHAPTER 19

Presence

❖ ❖ ❖

'Oh, it's you', Sir David grunted looking none too pleased. 'Where's your little friend George?'

'That's the point, isn't it, Sir?' Ned's manner was not polite. He leant forward and stared into Sir David's eyes. 'He's under arrest and under a wagon full of gunpowder'. This reply seemed to kindle something in Sir David.

'Don't get cheeky with me, young man!'

'Cheeky, cheeky', Ned repeated in his usual soft tones. Soft tones with just a little bit of menace though. He had his little pigsticker in Sir David's neck. The older man made a gobbling noise, but quietly too. It had all gone very quiet. Even the cries of the wounded, those being seen to by the barber-surgeons, hesitated to interfere. Another pause. 'You're going to help, Sir David'. And Ned waited for what seemed like hours as finally the spymaster nodded.

A few moments later and it was as if nothing had happened. Ned had to hand it to Sir David. There was no sign in his posture or his face that his life had just been threatened. There was one tiny spot of blood, slowly leaking into the ruffles of his white shirt. On a day like today, what was one drop of blood?

Perhaps five minutes passed as Ned explained what was needed. Ned could see the cogs of the spymaster's brain turning. 'You were quite right to threaten me, young Ned', he told the boy. 'I was testing you really. I'm sorry to have pushed you so far. However, that's your one free go. Don't ever let yourself do that again!'

There was a moment whilst they both thought about it. 'All right', Ned finally offered. And he left.

And so it was that a bizarre group of people assembled by the wall, by the wagon. Sir David on a litter (which a horse had initially dragged up the hill but then was propped up against the wall) nodded off in the late sun. George sat near him, under arrest but no longer under the wagon. It was a drumhead court martial. The angry Mr Granger strutted up and down in high boots and high dudgeon bellowing at the sky and the birds. Ned watched the man angrily too, like a cat that sees a mouse but can't get at it for the minute. Sir Ralph Hopton was clearly exhausted, the last thing he wanted was adjudicating between his spoilt nephew, to whom he could deny nothing, and the King's spymaster who outranked him in every possible way but whose existence was meant to be a secret.

Sir Hopton was lucky. The army was also exhausted. Nearly ten thousand men had collapsed over twenty acres, ignoring the dead bodies, and mostly asleep. There was a slow painful movement, like the oldest of old crones, gathering wood for camp fires, boiling water for stew, playing a penny whistle. Those who had not fought seemed to share the mood. They did not walk slowly but seemed tentative and gentle, offering beer or bandages for wounds. The whole made a gentle noise, like a herd of cows asleep, and the whole ignored the nephew and commander. Sir Hopton had posted pickets – sentries – to keep the common soldiers away but, for the moment, the common soldiers were far from interested.

Sir Hopton had his scribe, an annoying man in a moth-eaten black cloak, read back what had been said, again and again, as though repetition of the charge would in itself provide the answer. There was no answer. The whole thing would have to wait. Everyone knew. Except Mr Granger. He knew nothing except his own thwarted will. Every time he stamped angrily along the length of the wall, proceedings would stop. Most bored of all was the King's Executioner, summoned for this open and shut case that would not close. The pedantic voice of the clerk rose querulously again, much like the faint screaming of the swallows that dived and wheeled above the army, gorging on the flies that were everywhere.

Almost unnoticed, the enemy army left.

When brought the news (the event that made it officially a 'victory'), Sir Ralph Hopton had grown so bored he hardly managed a smile. His brigade commanders – three of them – were out watching the enemy or, in the case of Isaac Pendragith trying to re-occupy Bath. Nobody was there to cheer him up. He kept slurping down wine as dark as night and his mood slipped towards the same shade. And yet, it was a beautiful evening. He was still alive. He had beaten the Parliamentarians against every sort of odds.

It would be untrue to say that George was as bored as his commander. For starters, being on trial for your life tended to colour things. The beautiful evening was the beautiful evening when he might die. For all that, George was calm. Not befuddled, not particularly scared. He trusted Ned to save him and Sir David on a litter was still Sir David.

He stood happy enough with the threat of death hanging over him. He stood and felt a presence. Ned was the one for ghost and ghoulies. Ned loved nothing more than a witch's bone, talking dolls, haunted woods. George felt something now and he knew it meant something. He looked around. There were a few soldiers moving. One was adding a few more cuffs to the pile stripped from the enemy. The parliamentarians all wore a leather cuff with unit designations upon it. It was the only 'uniform' worn by any in this war and collecting the cuffs helped to work out enemy losses and placements. There was something about the man though. Was he crouching to disguise his height?

George checked all around to see if anyone else gave a strange twinge to him. No. It was only this man and when he turned again, the man had moved. A long way. He was now round the back of the wagon. Sir Hopton was pacing in front of it with his secretary. Sir David and Ned were propped up nearby.

'Ned get Sir David away now!' George shouted. He felt that his voice would have made Sam proud. Where was Sam? Thoughts twirled and sprinted through his thoughts like the dancers in a feverish masque. But his focus was razor-sharp on the creeping figure.

Sir Hopton looked askance as George moved towards the wagon. 'What what?' he gobbled – yes, George thought in the whirl of impressions, like a goose with his great feathery white shirt and the ridiculous feather in his hat. 'What are you doing Bowman?' he finally shouted, his red-face and double chins wobbling in disgust.

He knows my name George thought, amused at himself and the commander. George could see a tiny trail of smoke behind the wagon and, for a split second, the face of the man lighting a fuse. It was Scarface and Scarface was running, tumbling over the wall and George was shouting shouting shouting 'it's going to blow' over and over. Before the explosion, George spun in the air. He must have thrown himself one way or another. Time slowed to a crawl again – did this happen to everyone? George wondered. He himself was turning slowly in the air but his brain was still whizzing along.

He saw the summer sky. He saw the army laid out as though he were watching it from a furlong above it. He had time to admire the wisps of smoke. The whole battlefield – discarded weapons, patches of bright blood and duller gore, women moving slowly through the throng – like a model on a table open to his gaze. Thoughts of Catharine. Of Ned. Of his family back in High Ham. Of the hill above Langport and the shining Levels. The grand houses they had seen at Bradford. The bargees swearing on the river. Thoughts like flights of his own bright arrows. Thoughts of God. Thoughts of revenge on Scarface. Thoughts about the failings of his Commander...

And nothing.

Epilogue

❖ ❖ ❖

TWO DAYS LATER, NED WAS told that Sir Ralph Hopton had died. Ned had been one of the many soldiers milling round the tent, on and off for sixty hours, although his purposes were a little different. The mass of the soldiery were mourning the tragic ill-luck. 'What a shame!' they would say, again and a again as though repetition might add intelligence to the observation, as opposed to removing any that it might have had. 'The King's men's best commander'. 'Terrible accident'.

Ned had little else to do. He was finding it hard to sleep and he alternated hanging around Sir Hopton's death bed with hanging around Sir David's palette. To begin, the two men would have seemed to have the same sort of chances. But, like many of the horse races that Ned'd seen, it became clear that Sir David was pulling ahead and Sir Hopton pulling up. Ned had got Sir David out of the direct line of the blast but there had been a shower of wood, from wagon and barrels, which had struck both of them. Sir Hopton had, of course, flown into the air along with that other person.

One of the reasons why sleep eluded Ned was that every time he dropped off, there would be George's face. Ned would jerk awake sweating like a pig. Ned had tried everything – alcohol which he hated, a woman? The most he had managed was an hour. An hour of hideous nightmares. Ned wondered if it could be guilt. He really did not want to be going up to Weston Farm. He found Catharine unbearable.

Fighting – he'd done a lot of that. He had another fight arranged in an hour. Only when fighting did he stop feeling uncomfortable. Him, Ned Appleby, worrying over his life, his future! George would laugh if George was still around to laugh. Ned would have loved to talk to Ezekial. Another dead end. Another death.

Ned, of course, wished the army could have moved away, pursued the enemy, fought another real battle. But the army was slower than a housewife choosing a hat for a wedding as the saying had it.

Of course, unlike almost every other man in the army, Ned knew the actual numbers. The royalists had lost 2,500 men killed or badly wounded. The parliamentarians barely 400. That seemed less of a victory, in all honesty, and more of a defeat. However, it was not perhaps the truth that mattered, Ned thought. Everyone was excited and keen on the King's chances now. There were some who were already calling it the 'Royalist summer' although one battle hardly made it that, in Ned's view.

As had been happening often, Ned went from awake to troubled sleep in an eye-blink. In the dream, he was at the wall

with George. He looked back and watched the muskets and cal-
livers fire. In the dream it was night-time and a mis-fire – the
so-called flash in the pan – lit up the faces and the smoke. The
noise was insane, like some mighty engine hammering bang
bang bang. And then there was Ezekial. 'Ezekial', he shouted in
the dream and the noise stopped. Easy hovered over the battlefield and the soldiers frozen like statues and the smoke frozen
and even the light frozen. And Ned knew, even in his dream-
ing, that he'd only get the one chance to ask. Luckily, he knew
what to ask. 'Will you help me Ezekial?' he demanded.

'You're the king now', Ezekial replied.

And Ned woke again. Not really a sleep. A moment unconscious. Ned wondered if there was a name for this strange
falling asleep. He then wondered how his mind could make the
fight at the wall into a night-time engagement. Or was it like
the witches said – dreams told you the future. Despite what
George had always thought, Ned didn't believe in witch-craft,
in the super-natural as the vicar called it, using another of his
new words. He loved the new words, the vicar did. No, Ned
hated witchcraft.

And then Ned thought about what the dream Ezekial had
said. Ned had spent hours talking to Ezekial. In fact, he had
never spoken to anyone like he had talked to the charcoal-
burner, which still meant that Easy had done most of the talking.
One of the ways that Ned had 'talked' was by Easy reading his
mind. 'You'll be thinking that I've lost me marbles', he'd say
and almost every time, he'd be right. It turned out that Ezekial
claimed to be the 'king of the charcoal burners'. Considering

how few there were left, this did not add up to much more than a hill of beans. Ezekial never quite told Ned what being the king meant. It was too late to ask Ezekial in real life.

Ned had been the one to find the charcoal burner, the king. He was impaled on top of his charcoal clamp with a pike. The ash of the pike had, when Ned found him, burnt through to charcoal. Easy had been still alive. Ned had carefully taken him off the clamp, Easy's clothes lightly charred and Easy's body even more smoked than before. Ned had started to take off some of the layers – leather baked to a thin crisp, linen scorched dark brown.

'Put me back and burn me', Easy had said – his last words in fact although it was a few hours until his last breath had left his body. While Ned sat there, the old man's exhalations slowing to an occasional gasp and Ned giving him tiny sips of Weston spring water, the murderers had returned to the copse. Ned could hear them, crashing around and shouting in London accents. They had failed to even find the clearing. Ned did not think they would necessarily have harmed him – a small boy cradling a dying charcoal-burner – and he himself felt a certain weariness. Perhaps he would not have killed them. However, their names and their banter, he was going to remember – Isaac, Temperance, Forthright, Plunge. Ned presumed that they were religious types – non-conformists, low church. Possibly familists. Ned did not know enough about the myriad of sects swarming in the Parliamentary army like mosquito larvae in a bucket of water.

They crashed away again, having discussed Ezekial in ways that made Ned icily rage. In fact, every fight he had made him remember ITFP, as he called them. He wondered, of course, if any were Scarface, the voices were similar but then the rebel army was full of Londoners or Midlanders.

Ned lost the fight that night.

Printed in Great Britain
by Amazon